# GYPSY SERENADE

## BY
## SANDY COCCIA

ISBN (softcover): 979-8-9862355-0-9

ISBN (Kindle):  979-8-9862355-1-6

# DEDICATION

*Dedicated to all the creative people in this world who go against what they should be doing and are brave enough to do what they are passionate about! Keep on bringing your music, colors, art, and dance to the world.*

*Dedicated to my kind and amazing husband, Clayton, and because of him, I have the freedom to be a full-time writer, filmmaker, and artist.*

"LET THE MUSIC OPEN YOUR HEART

LET THE COLORS BRING YOU LIFE

LET THE DANCE SET YOU FREE"

# PROLOGUE

~ 5 ~

Shoulders hunched beneath his oversized coat; the old man shuffled through the cemetery gates. Dark glasses hid his eyes, while a wide-brimmed hat cast his face in shadow. He navigated the labyrinth of marble and granite with the certainty of a decade's practice until he reached a modest white marker nestled under a lone oak.

His arthritic knees protested as he lowered himself to the ground. Weathered fingers brushed away fallen leaves and twigs from the stone's surface.

"Jó napot, kedvesem," he murmured.

"The sky is clear today—you must have a beautiful view." His gaze drifted upward before returning to the grave. "Still empty without you." From his pocket came four blossoms: twin white violets paired with purple dwarf irises, their yellow centers bright against the stone.

"Te vagy a gyönyörű finom virágom, szeretlek," he whispered, then added softly, "You are my beautiful, delicate flower. I love you."

His lips brushed the cool marble.

"Until next Tuesday, then."

# CHAPTER 1

Fiddles wailed and tambourines shimmered beneath stained-glass windows that fractured moonlight into jeweled patterns across the tavern floor. The Romani bar pulsed with life—glasses clinked, laughter erupted, and conversations swelled like the tide. Men with open-throated shirts and gold earrings leaned across tables where women draped in vibrant fabrics and jingling silver bracelets tossed their heads back in delight, their bohemian spirit as intoxicating as the amber liquor flowing freely from bottle to glass.

On a stage at the room's center, a Romani woman danced, her black hair whipping around her shoulders, her skirt flaring like flames against the dim light. Charles paused at the door, loosening his tie. His polished oxfords and pressed slacks marked him as out of place—a raven among peacocks. Transfixed, his briefcase dangled forgotten until he stumbled backward into a wall of muscle. Amber liquid splashed across tattooed forearms.

"Watch yourself, outsider," the man growled, bunching Charles's collar in his fist.

Viola leapt between them, her bracelets clattering as she pressed a hand against the larger man's chest.

"Vlad, enough. He's a guest." Her eyes, still bright from dancing, found Charles. "You're not hurt?"

Charles straightened, unable to look away. "Better than I've been in years. Let me replace that drink—for both of you."

# CHAPTER 2

Night after night, Charles returned to the bar, drawn by Viola's magnetic presence. With each visit, the space between them narrowed—her hand lingering longer on his arm, their whispered conversations growing more intimate, their shared drinks becoming a ritual of trust.

When she pulled him onto the dance floor, his banker's rigidity melted away beneath her guidance, his body finding rhythms he never knew it possessed. Their joy echoed through the tavern, harmonizing with the fiddles' plaintive cry.

From the shadows, men with gleaming earrings and bare forearms watched, their expressions hardening with each shared smile. The moment Viola disappeared to the bar, Charles felt himself wrenched backward into darkness, the rough brick wall greeting his spine with a painful crack.

Through the ring of snarling faces came Viola's voice, sharp as a blade.

"Let him go! He's mine!"

Charles tasted copper as Vlad's scarred knuckles clenched.

"He wears our welcome thin," Vlad spat. "Your blood deserves better."

Viola's chin lifted, her earrings catching lamplight like twin moons.

"My heart chooses him. I'll walk between our world and his."

She crossed over to Charles through the circle of scowling men, her gaze never leaving his. The tavern's noise fell away as she reached for his bruised face, her fingertips gentle against his jaw.

Charles drew her close, his banker's restraint dissolving as her warmth pressed against him. Their lips met with the hunger of worlds colliding, sealing a promise neither had spoken aloud.

# CHAPTER 3

Charles slipped through the revolving doors of Barclay International Bank before dawn touched the skyscraper's highest windows. His oxfords clicked against marble as cleaning crews buffed floors beneath brass sconces. In his corner office, he poured coffee black as midnight into bone china and thumbed through bond prospectuses with practiced precision.

By ten, he stood before senior partners, his voice steady as he outlined profit margins while sunlight caught the citrus polish on the oak paneling. Emmett Raptnor's hand fell heavy on his shoulder. "Stellar work."

Back at his desk, Charles stared at Viola's message the secretary had left: *"Meet me at The Crimson Lantern?"*

Charles was torn between his work and meeting Viola. He adjusted his cufflinks and strode toward the Everleigh Club luncheon, where crystal chandeliers refracted light across white tablecloths. The handle of his briefcase grew slick in his grip as china clinked around him. Between bites of untouched salmon, Viola's face floated before him.

He rose suddenly, crossing to Raptnor's table.

"Emmett, I need to finish something at home. May I be excused?"

Raptnor nodded, pleased by such dedication. "By all means."

Charles's hand trembled as he slipped the velvet box into his jacket pocket, the weight of it pulling at the fabric.

# CHAPTER 4

The Gypsy bar's neon sign flickered against Viola's bare shoulders as she stepped outside, her flowered dress catching the evening breeze. The wicker picnic basket creaked in his grip while they walked in silence to the stone bridge where they had first kissed.

Wine glasses clinked as he spread the blanket over grass still warm from the afternoon sun. Viola's fingers brushed his as she accepted a slice of aged gouda, her silver bracelets jingling. The city lights reflected in her eyes when he finally reached into his pocket.

The diamond caught fire in the twilight as he opened the box, his voice barely audible above the rushing water below.

"Between your world and mine, there's room for us to build our own. Marry me, and let's build that world together."

Viola's eyes widened, her lips parting slightly as she stared at the diamond. Her silver bracelets jangled when she reached toward the ring, then pulled back. She bit her lower lip, gaze darting between Charles and the city lights beyond the bridge. A breath, then her face softened.

"Yes," she whispered, then louder, "Yes!"

Her hands trembled as Charles slid the ring onto her finger. The diamond caught the neon glow from distant signs as he lifted her hand to his lips. Their foreheads touched, breath mingling in the cool evening air, until Viola pressed her palm against his chest, creating space between them.

"My father," she said, twisting the new ring on her finger. "We need his blessing."

Charles nodded once, firmly, his jaw set with determination.

# *CHAPTER 5*

Viola's silver bracelets jingled as she pushed open the weathered oak door of the little stone cottage. Pebbled walkways wound through fairy-tale gardens where crimson poppies and indigo morning glories tangled with herbs. The rich aroma of cabbage, potatoes, and sizzling bacon wafted from the doorway, enveloping her childhood memories.

"Papa? Papa, where are you?" she called, her voice echoing against the copper pots hanging from rough-hewn ceiling beams.

Milosh emerged from the kitchen, his salt-and-pepper mustache drooping over a wide smile. Colorful embroidery adorned his traditional vest, which strained slightly over his barrel chest.

"My daughter, Viola! The sun itself couldn't brighten this day more than your face." His calloused hands clasped hers. "What brings you here? No, no—it doesn't matter. Stay, have some porridge and fruit; the blackberries were picked this morning."

He enfolded her in a hearty hug that smelled of pipe tobacco and spices. Viola pulled back, fingers trembling.

"Papa, there's something I need to tell you..." Her words faltered as she extended her slender arm, the diamond catching the firelight from the hearth. "I'm engaged!"

Milosh's bushy eyebrows shot upward, joy and surprise dancing across his deeply lined face.

"My heart sings! But which lucky man have you chosen?" His eyes twinkled, clearly picturing the many Romani suitors who had danced in attendance on his daughter.

Viola's gaze dropped to the worn carpet beneath her feet.

"He isn't a gypsy, Papa. His name is Charles. He's a banker—with gentle hands and honest eyes. I love him more than any man I've known."

Milosh's smile dimmed as he stroked his beard, crow's feet deepening around his eyes.

"What does this mean? Will this outsider understand our ways? Will our Viola vanish into his world of stone and glass?"

His gaze lifted to his daughter's face, which glowed with an inner light he couldn't deny.

"Then I must meet this man who has stolen my daughter's heart!"

"Good," Viola whispered, gesturing toward the beaded curtain that separated the front room from the entryway. "Because he's here now."

Charles ducked beneath the low doorframe, his tailored suit at odds with the cottage's rustic beams.

"Mr. Borza, it's an honor to—"

Milosh's weathered hand closed around his elbow, guiding him past copper pots and dried herbs into a small back room where family portraits crowded the walls.

"My daughter is not some bauble," Milosh said, his accent thickening with emotion. "She is our treasure, our little flower."

Charles straightened his cuffs, a practiced gesture.

"Sir, I'll give her a life of security—fine things, a proper home."

Milosh's fingers trembled against his embroidered vest as he studied the banker's polished shoes. Finally, he nodded once, a patriarch's blessing heavy with sacrifice. No contract needed signing; the exchange of a daughter had been negotiated in the ancient way of men.

# CHAPTER 6

Two years later, Camilla arrived with her mother's raven curls and her father's sea-glass green eyes. On weekends, Charles would loosen his banker's tie to push her on the garden swing while Viola watched from the stone bench he had installed beside her herb garden.

The pebbled pathway wound through roses and morning glories—echoes of the childhood home she had left behind. Sometimes at dusk, when Charles returned from the office with his briefcase still in hand, he would find them both beneath the oak tree, Viola's silver bracelets catching the fading light as she spun their daughter to the crackling violin music from the phonograph.

In those moments, watching his wife's colorful skirts twirl as Camilla's laughter bubbled up toward the darkening sky, Charles would join in—dancing with Viola as he had at the gypsy bar—and then lift little Camilla, swinging her around to the music. At that moment, Charles felt the walls between their worlds dissolve completely.

This perfect world would soon be interrupted. As Charles's office hours lengthened with each promotion, Viola poured herself into motherhood, teaching Camilla the dances of her ancestors. Yet beneath her silver bracelets, a familiar restlessness stirred. Camilla's life was filled with color, music, and dance. Their days flowed in a rhythm of bedtime stories and violin lessons, of herbs growing alongside roses—until the moment their carefully balanced world shattered like crystal against stone, and everything came crashing down.

# CHAPTER 7

Camilla, now a young girl of ten, lay on her side in an oversized bed, surrounded by fluffy embroidered pillows and silk sheets tucked tightly around her tiny body. Her long, shiny black hair draped across her shoulders, forming a striking contrast against the white lace bedcovers. Her eyes, usually emerald green, were now clouded with a smoky tint.

As tears slipped down her pale ivory skin, she stared at the farthest wall of the room. There, tucked in the corner, rested a finely crafted violin, elegantly carved with mother-of-pearl inlaid flowers along its base. The violin's varnish glowed a rich burnt orange, except for the barber-pole inlaid purfling, which shimmered an iridescent ebony. Her gaze traced the beautiful instrument—from the meticulously carved base, up the perfectly strung neck—until it caught on a large crack running down the middle, leaving the top of the instrument hanging limply to one side.

The once-perfect violin, made with the deepest love and passed through generations into her hands, now lay crippled and lifeless.

Caught in the shock of what she saw, her tears flowed harder. She whispered under her breath, "Daddy, why?"

Distracted by her emotions, she didn't notice the door opening or her father walking toward her.

"Hey, honey, are you still awake?" he asked, settling down beside her on the bed.

She turned her head away to avoid his gaze, hoping he hadn't heard her whisper. He tried to hug her, but she pulled away. Persistent, he gently brushed her hair from her face, leaning over to kiss her cheek. His effort met with more resistance as she curled up tightly, inching as far away as she could.

"Camilla, please look at me. I'm sorry about the violin." Losing patience, he reached over and gripped her left shoulder.

"Ouch! You're hurting me!" she cried.

"Listen, I'll get your toy fixed tomorrow!" Her tears only made him angrier.

Camilla turned her face toward him, summoning all the courage her small body could muster.

"It's not a toy. Mommy gave it to me—it's not a toy!"

Grabbing both her shoulders, he shook her roughly.

"Stop it! Stop it! I will not lose you too. I won't let you waste your time on that—"

He stopped mid-sentence, forced himself to breathe, and slowly loosened his grip.

Gently, he pried her fingers from the violin's neck one by one and slid her worn teddy bear into her empty hand, closing her small fingers around its plush body.

"Listen, honey, I will take your violin to Mr. Hempshaw tomorrow. He will fix it for you, and everything will be okay again. All right?"

He tried his best to soothe her, but it didn't matter. For Camilla, the damage was already done.

She looked at her father with a blank, empty stare. He was a stranger now frightening yet commanding her obedience. Not wanting more trouble, she simply nodded.

"Okay, Daddy."

"That's my good little girl. Now go to sleep."

He reached over, kissed her forehead, and pulled the blanket up around her small frame.

As he walked out, he felt the urge to explain, to comfort her, but instead he turned at the door. "We only have each other now. That's all we have, Camilla. Good night, daughter."

Camilla said nothing. She rolled away, curling toward the wall where her broken violin lay in its open case, the fractured neck visible even in the dim light. Her eyes never left it.

"It's all I have left of you, Mommy. All I have left is my Johnnii," she whispered, drifting off to sleep.

# CHAPTER 8

**TEN YEARS LATER**

Camilla lay in her large canopy bed, staring toward the corner of her room. Her hair was still long and shiny black, now feathered stylishly and resting against her alabaster skin. Despite how striking her hair and complexion were, her most captivating feature were her eyes—an unusual, bright green that seemed like open windows to her soul.

There, in the corner, lay her violin in the same position as always. The shiny maple had dulled, and the soft velvet lining of the case was dustier now. Nothing had changed—it was still broken, still lying limply to one side. The violin was the first thing she saw every morning and the last thing she looked at each night, day after day for the past ten years.

Despite her father's repeated arguments—telling her to "get rid of that piece of junk"—she always replied, "When are you going to take it to Mr. Hempshaw to get it repaired, as you promised?" Each time, their conversations ended the same way: angry words, slammed doors, and silence.

Her thoughts drifted to their last argument—one of the loudest and most violent. It happened just yesterday, as her father prepared to leave for work. Now the president and CEO of the largest bank in town, Global Bank and Trust, Charles Huntington enjoyed the title, prestige, and wealth his position offered. His success provided every comfort: a grand house, the best private schooling, and a glittering social life.

But as much as he tried to buy her happiness, all the money in the world could not fill the void in his daughter's heart. She still clung to the simple, broken violin more than anything he could offer.

They often fought over values and priorities, careers, independence, and the past—but every dispute circled back to the violin. If only she would "grow up and stop hanging on to that toy," he would say. Then came the shouting, the slammed doors, and the heavy silence that followed. Later, they would find each other again, trade polite apologies, and never touch the real pain between them.

# CHAPTER 9

Michael Smithers had worked for Charles Huntington since the beginning of his banking career. They had been partners for years, and Michael was close to Charles's family. His young daughter, Camilla, even called him "Uncle Michael," though they were not related by blood.

Despite their long partnership, Michael and Charles differed greatly in how they conducted business.

Michael was a cocky young man, consumed by ambition and driven by greed. He was relentless on his path to success in the ruthless world of finance, willing to do whatever it took to get to the top—even if it meant stepping over anyone in his way. His hunger for power drew him into questionable company: petty thieves and small-time criminals at first, but as his wealth and position grew, so did his associates. The petty criminals were replaced by far more dangerous men—low-life criminals disguised as legitimate businessmen in Armani suits and Alessandro Démesure alligator leather shoes.

On a cold but sunny Monday morning, a dramatic turn of events was about to change the direction of Michael's career—propelling him to new heights professionally while sending his moral character into a steep decline.

Michael sat in his office, his usual morning coffee steaming beside his appointment book. As he flipped through his planner, his secretary, Ms. Carolyn Terrance, burst into the room looking flustered.

"Sir, there's a gentleman who wishes to speak with you," she said quietly.

"On the phone, Carolyn?" Michael asked.

"No, sir—he's outside your office," she replied.

Michael frowned and glanced at his schedule. "I don't see any appointment until ten a.m. Have him make one and come back at a scheduled time. I am too busy."

"Um, sir, you don't understand..." Before she could finish, the door flew open. Two large men entered, followed by a distinguished-looking older man wearing an Armani suit and Alessandro Démesure alligator shoes.

They brushed Ms. Terrance aside. "Excuse us, miss. We'll take it from here. Please bring Mr. Sergio a hot cup of coffee—porcelain cup, no paper. Understood?" said the first henchman.

Carolyn looked to Michael for confirmation. He nodded stiffly.

"Yes, of course. Carolyn, bring a whole fresh pot and four cups."

He turned to the older man. "Very kind, Mr. Smithers. Yes, four cups," the man said, sitting down confidently. His demeanor made it clear he was in charge.

When Carolyn left and the door closed, the two men took up guard positions at the entrance.

Michael cleared his throat. "How may I help you, Mr....?"

"So sorry—let me introduce myself. I am Sergio Joaquin Morelia. I have a large sum of money and will be opening an account here at your bank," he said in a commanding tone.

"Of course, Mr. Morelia," Michael replied, extending his hand.

Sergio grasped it firmly, placing his other hand beneath Michael's elbow as he shook. "I was told by my associates that you are the banker—and this is the bank—that will take good care of me. Is that true, Mr. Smithers?"

"Yes, certainly. I'd love to have you as a client. I'll just need to fill out the standard application and have my compliance department confirm your information and—"

Michael stopped short as Sergio raised a hand to silence him.

"Oh no, you misunderstand, Mr. Smithers. May I call you Michael?"

Michael nodded cautiously.

"You see, Michael, I'm a businessman—imports and exports, cash business. I have a great deal of influence in this town and know many people... some mutual friends of yours, I believe. I was told you could expedite my file—bypass all this application nonsense and paperwork."

Michael swallowed. "Well, Mr. Morelia, I'm only the vice president. There are certain protocols I have to follow. You understand, right?"

Sergio smiled thinly. "No, I don't understand at all. I was told by my associates—Mr. James Gianni, Mr. Sam Biamonti, and their boss, Mr. Antonio Cervantes—that you're *the man* who knows how to keep things confidential. And they, of course, are willing to keep your confidentiality in return. Now, is that clear?"

Standing up, Sergio leaned over the desk, his eyes hard.

Michael's mind spun from fear to regret, but his face broke into a mechanical smile. "Yes, of course. You come with excellent recommendations. I am sure I can shorten the paperwork and get your account approved immediately."

"Good." Sergio leaned back, satisfied. "Now—where's that coffee? I'd like a cup while you complete my account." He gestured to one of his men. "Go find Ms. Terrance and see what's taking so long."

Moments later, Carolyn returned with a silver tray holding a steaming pot of coffee, four porcelain cups, and a plate of freshly baked cookies.

"I thought you might like some cookies too," she said sweetly. "I made them fresh this morning."

"Why, thank you, Carolyn. Now *that* is service!" Sergio smiled broadly, taking a cup and a cookie before settling in.

Within the hour, Michael was shaking hands and escorting Sergio out of his office. The older man carried a folder containing two newly formed checking accounts and a savings account—all approved and ready for the large deposits that would follow.

As months passed and Sergio's balance grew, Michael found himself opening several more accounts—for Mr. Fuentes, Mr. Guzman, and Mr. Lorenzo—all in the "import-export" business.

Michael's newfound success did not go unnoticed by Charles. As long as Michael brought in results, Charles was content to turn a blind eye.

# CHAPTER 10



Carolyn walked up to the office door with a box of freshly baked cookies under one arm and a stack of mail under the other. Balancing everything, she fumbled with her keys, struggling to unlock the door as the desk phone rang inside. The ringing stopped, then started again, continuing for several minutes until she finally managed to open the door.

Running inside, she quickly dropped everything onto her desk—her neatly stacked pyramid of mail and cookies toppling over. She snatched up the phone receiver, slightly out of breath.

"Good morning, Mr. Smithers's office. Carolyn Terrance speaking."

The familiar voice on the other end replied, "Good morning, Carolyn. Are you all right? You sound winded."

"Oh yes, Mr. Huntington, thank you. What can I do for you?"

"I need Michael to come to my office the minute he arrives. Understood?"

"Yes, sir." She glanced at the doorway just as Michael walked in. "Oh—here he is now. I will send him right over."

Michael raised an eyebrow. "What's going on? Quite early for so much commotion."

"I don't know. Mr. Huntington wants you immediately in his office."

"Okay."

As Michael headed to the elevator, nervous thoughts filled his mind. *I wonder what the urgency is… Hope everything's all right.*

He took a deep breath, straightened his tie, brushed back his hair, and walked into Charles's large office suite.

Inside the reception area, Charles's secretary, Sylvia, immediately stood and ushered him into the main office.

Charles sat at his desk, phone in hand, looking intense. He motioned for Michael to sit while finishing his call. "Yes, yes, he's here now. We'll talk soon. Great—I'll have Sylvia set up a lunch. Thank you." He pressed a few buttons. "Sylvia, I have Mr. Raptnor on the line. Please schedule a lunch meeting as soon as possible—clear my calendar."

Charles hung up, got up from his chair, and surprised Michael by giving him a hearty hug.

"Michael! My boy—my wonder boy!"

"Wow, Charles," Michael replied, smiling awkwardly. "Why such a warm greeting?"

"You deserve it! Do you know who I was just on the phone with?"

Before Michael could respond, Charles continued excitedly, "Mr. Emmett Raptnor—the CEO of Barclay International Bank, the largest financial institution in the world. Offices in London, Singapore, New York—over four thousand branches in sixty countries!"

"Yes, I've heard of them," Michael said carefully. "What does that have to do with us?"

Charles grinned. "You know I used to work for him, right? He was my mentor—taught me everything I know, good, bad, and ugly."

"Of course," Michael said with a wink.

Charles continued, practically glowing with excitement. "They want to discuss a merger! A merger with our small bank! Thanks to you and the high-profile clients you've brought in, our assets have grown from millions to billions."

Michael froze for a moment, his stomach tightening. Forcing a smile, he said, "Wow—amazing. That's... great news."

As Charles continued talking, Michael barely heard a word. His mind raced through all the accounts he had opened—billions of dollars in laundered money. *What am I going to do when they look into this?* Then, almost as quickly, a cold realization settled over him. *Charles is the CEO. He's responsible for everything. If anyone asks, I'll point to him.*

A slow smile spread across his face. Charles noticed and assumed it was joy.

"Michael," Charles said, clapping him on the back, "you've earned this. You're a big reason we're in this position."

Michael leaned forward, his tone steady but his words calculated. "Charles, let's not forget who signed off on all those accounts."

Charles arched with an eyebrow. "You're not concerned about our new clients, are you?"

"Just making sure we're on the same page," Michael replied smoothly. "After all, you met every one of those gentlemen personally."

Charles waved a dismissive hand. "Yes, yes—all proper introductions. Nothing to worry about."

"Great," Michael said, forcing a grin. "Let's get ready for that lunch meeting."

# CHAPTER 11

Visitors who wandered into the Hempshaw Instrument Repair Shop often felt as though they had stepped back in time. The cluttered little store on the corner of Fifth and Main exuded old-world charm. Its owner always sat in the same chair, a small bright light illuminating his work as he hunched over a broken instrument, repairing it with the precision of a fine jeweler.

No matter how busy he was, Loiza Hempshaw always stopped to talk with his customers, regaling them with stories of the many famous instruments he had restored. Each story came alive with the intricate details and memories he recalled so vividly.

"Please, call me Louie—it's more American," he would tell people in his heavy Hungarian accent. And then, as always, he'd talk to each customer like they were an old friend from the old country.

That morning, Camilla stood outside the shop, hesitant to go in. She peered through the window, hearing faint violin music that seemed to grow louder the longer she listened. She looked down at the violin case in her hand, nodded resolutely, and pushed open the door.

Camilla was in no mood for small talk. She wanted to get this over with—like pulling off a bandage before it hurt too much.

"Mr. Hempshaw," she called quickly as she approached the workbench.

The old man looked up, smiling. "Why, good morning, my dear! What a pleasant surprise. How can I—"

She cut him off, her voice rushed and uneven from nerves and lack of sleep. "Here is my violin. I'd like to sell it, but my father said I should get it appraised first."

"Well, let's see what we have here," Mr. Hempshaw said, gently opening the case as Camilla continued to speak.

"You see, it's damaged beyond repair. The sound—it's gone. I kept it locked away for so long because..." Her voice cracked. Tears blurred her vision as she clutched the violin to her chest. The shop around her seemed to dissolve, replaced by the memory of her mother's face—those deep brown eyes filled with warmth and sorrow, framed by raven hair that caught the light even on the darkest days.

Mr. Hempshaw carefully took the violin from her trembling hands. As the lid creaked open, a cloud of fine dust rose and caught the sunlight, glittering like tiny stars. For a moment, the motes of dust seemed to form a feminine silhouette before fading back into the air.

A whisper echoed faintly through the shop, so delicate it might have been the sigh of the case hinge:

*Let the music open your heart.*

The melody pulsed through Camilla's fingertips, spreading into her chest. Her gaze fell on the violin—her confidant from childhood—its deep crack a wound that never healed.

The maple wood still gleamed beneath years of neglect; the scroll still curled gracefully at the top.

"Johnnii," she whispered—the childhood name catching in her throat. The room tilted, her mother's voice and the haunting melody swirling around her. Her knees gave way.

Before she hit the floor, strong hands caught her mid-fall.

"Steady there," a deep voice said as arms encircled her waist, lifting her gently upright. "Are you okay?"

Camilla opened her eyes to see the face of a handsome young man—ethereal, with a faint beard, soft brown eyes framed by long lashes, and a wisp of light brown hair falling into his face. Concern softened his features, then turned into a warm smile as she regained color.

"Oh, good—you look better now," he said. "Got some color back in your cheeks. Let me help you up."

He steadied her, still holding her lightly. Noticing her tight grip on the violin case, he nodded toward it. "Must be very important to you?"

"Wha... what..." she stammered, still disoriented. Regaining her composure, she loosened her grip and placed the violin back on the counter. "Mr. Hempshaw, please—I'd like you to appraise it and sell it."

He looked at her over his glasses. "Oh, certainly. I will fix it for you—make it like new."

"No, no, you misunderstand me." Her tone wavered. "This is for you to keep. I no longer want it. Please, Mr. Hempshaw—no questions. I must sell it."

"Well... all right," he said, curiosity flickering in his eyes. "It's such a beautiful piece. Can you give me an hour? I have a couple of other repairs to finish first."

"Thank you," she said softly.

Remembering her manners, Camilla turned to the young man. "And thank you—for helping me. That was very kind."

"No problem. Are you sure you're alright? That was quite a fall," he said, concern lingering in his voice.

But Camilla, still lightheaded, only managed to make a polite smile before turning toward the door. She needed air. The moment she stepped outside, the cold wind hit her face. Queasy and trembling, she decided to stop at the little coffee shop next door.

# CHAPTER 12

The coffee shop was small but inviting, its interior filled with the scent of roasted beans and freshly baked pastries. Camilla took a seat by the window, hoping the quiet hum of conversation would calm her spinning thoughts. Her hands still trembled slightly as she wrapped them around a warm cup of cappuccino, its steam curling upward like wisps of memory.

Outside, the morning sun had risen fully, glinting off passing cars and shop windows. Life went on as usual—people hurrying to work, laughter spilling from the bakery across the street. Yet to Camilla, the world felt muted, like a song playing in a language she could no longer understand.

She stared into the milky foam, watching it swirl, then fade. Her mother's voice echoed faintly in her mind—soft, melodic, filled with love.

*Let the music open your heart.*

The words haunted her. For years, she had buried them beneath the noise of her father's ambition and her own pain. Selling the violin was supposed to free her from the past, but instead it made her feel hollow, as if she were betraying something sacred.

She looked out the window again—and froze.

Across the street, standing in front of Hempshaw's shop window, was the same young man who had caught her when she fainted. He was holding the violin. The sunlight shimmered across its cracked body, making the damaged wood gleam like gold.

He turned slightly, meeting her gaze through the glass. For a moment, the busy street seemed to fall away, leaving only the two of them locked in silent recognition. Then he smiled—a calm, knowing smile—and disappeared back into the shop.

Camilla's heart thudded painfully in her chest. Something in that moment—his eyes, the way he handled the violin—felt both familiar and impossible.

Without thinking, she stood, leaving her coffee untouched, and rushed back across the street. The bell above the door jingled as she pushed it open, her breath coming in quick bursts.

"Mr. Hempshaw!" she called. "The man—where is he?"

The old craftsman looked up from his workbench, puzzled. "What man, my dear?"

"The one who helped me earlier. The one with the violin!"

Mr. Hempshaw tilted his head. "I've been alone since you left. Perhaps you saw someone outside?"

Camilla's stomach twisted. "No... I saw him in here. He had my violin."

Mr. Hempshaw frowned slightly and opened the case still sitting on the counter. The violin was inside—cracked, untouched, exactly as she had left it.

Camilla stepped back, confusion flashing across her face. "But... I saw..." Her voice trailed off.

Mr. Hempshaw smiled gently, his eyes kind. "Perhaps your heart is trying to tell you something." He picked up the violin and plucked one of the unbroken strings. The faint, trembling note filled the air. "Even the most wounded instrument can sing again."

Camilla blinked, the tension in her chest easing just a little. "Maybe you're right."

"Of course I'm right," he said with a wink. "Now, go get yourself some rest. Come back tomorrow. We'll see what we can do for your old friend."

As she left the shop, Camilla glanced once more through the window—half expecting to see the mysterious young man again. But he was gone. Only the violin remained, glinting faintly beneath the workshop light, as if waiting for her to return.

# CHAPTER 13

The next morning arrived cloaked in fog, the kind that softened the city's edges and blurred the line between waking and dream. Camilla moved quickly through the damp streets, her boots splashing through shallow puddles. She hadn't slept at all. Her mind replayed the image of the violin, its faint glow, and the echo of her mother's voice whispering through the air like a melody half remembered.

When she reached Hempshaw's shop, the little bell above the door stayed silent. The window display was dark, and a hand-lettered sign hung crookedly in the glass:

**"Closed for Inventory."**

Camilla's shoulders sank. She pressed her palm against the cool windowpane and peered inside. The violin still rested on the counter where she had left it, the light catching its polished surface as if something inside it still breathed.

"Please," she whispered, her breath fogging the glass. "Don't fade again."

"Talking to ghosts already?"

The voice startled her. She turned to see a young man standing near the side entrance, a few paint smudges across his shirt and hands. His hair was tousled, his expression kind.

"I didn't mean to scare you," he said quickly. "I live upstairs. I'm a painter."

Camilla blinked. "You live here?"

He nodded. "Yeah. Name's Johnny."

The name hit her like a soft note struck on a familiar string. *Johnny.*

"I saw you yesterday," he continued. "remember the knight in shining armour who kept you from kissing the cold tile floor?" he said with a chuckle but Camilla was lost in her own thoughts barely paying attention.

"You looked like you'd lost something important." He said

"I did," Camilla said quietly. "My mother... and that violin."

Johnny stepped closer, wiping his hands on a paint-stained cloth. "Mr. Hempshaw brought it in last night. I saw it—beautiful piece. Feels alive, somehow."

Camilla's breath caught. "You can feel that too?"

He nodded, his gaze steady. "I can see it. The soul inside things— the light people carry, even when they've forgotten it's there."

For the first time in years, she didn't feel alone in her grief.

"Would you like to see it again?" he asked.

She nodded.

Johnny unlocked the door and led her inside. The air felt warm, humming faintly—as if the world was holding its breath. Dust motes drifted through the sunlight, glowing softly around them.

The violin sat on the counter.

Johnny handed it to her gently. "Go on."

Her fingers trembled as she lifted it. The moment her skin brushed the wood, a vibration rippled through her—a pulse of warmth that spread through her chest.

Then came a whisper.

Her mother's voice.

*Let the music open your heart.*

Camilla froze. "Mom?" she whispered.

The light around her mother brightened, her smile glowing with pride. Her hand—made of light and memory—brushed Camilla's cheek. "*Let the music open your heart.*"

When Camilla opened her eyes, her mother's spirit was gone—but the warmth remained. The shop was quiet again, grounded in the stillness after something holy.

Johnny's hand rested lightly on her shoulder. "You okay?" he asked.

She nodded slowly, wiping her tears. "Yes," she whispered. "I think I am."

Camilla gazed down at the violin. Its surface shimmered softly, whole once more. A tremulous smile broke through her tears as she whispered the words that had brought her mother back.

"*Let the music open your heart.*"

For a moment, she stood motionless, lost in the stillness of the room and the echo of her own voice. Then Johnny's gentle words pulled her from the spell.

"Oh—sorry," she murmured, blinking rapidly. "It's just... a lot to take in. I should leave Mr. Hempshaw a note, let him know I saw the violin. He's not quite finished with his appraisal, so I'll come back tomorrow."

She reached for a slip of paper and began to write, but Johnny's voice stopped her.

"Wait—before you go, how about a cup of coffee?"

She smiled faintly. "Oh no, I really should get home."

"It's early," he said, his tone warm and coaxing. "Coffee shop is just across the street"

"oh yes" Camilla remembering her brief visit there yesterday

"And doesn't a fresh cup of coffee sound perfect on a morning like this?" Johnny continued

Camilla hesitated, then relented. With a small nod, she placed the violin carefully back in its case and let Johnny escort her out into the crisp morning air.

# CHAPTER 14

The mahogany-paneled dining room glowed with amber light, crystal catching the flicker of candle flames as waiters moved in a choreography of quiet precision. Burgundy breathed in wide-bellied glasses; silver domes rose and fell like a tide.

At the head of the table sat Mr. Emmett Raptnor—relaxed, assured, the room orbiting him. He didn't so much command attention as make it inevitable. When he spoke, conversations thinned to a hush.

Charles sat several seats down, posture tall, smile polished. It felt like fortune itself had drawn out the chair for him. Raptnor's team had moved with shocking speed, and the "green light" for a merger came faster than Charles dared hope. He tried to wear the look of a man accustomed to such rooms, but inside he felt like a boy who had slipped into the orchestra and found himself suddenly keeping time.

Across from him, Michael Smithers rotated the burgundy in his glass, expression bland. Beneath it: static. He knew the money that had swelled their books had not all come scrubbed and sanctified. Raptnor's due diligence was legend. For it to pass this quickly meant one of two things—someone missed the stains, or someone decided stains were an acceptable color.

Raptnor lifted his glass, voice smooth as the wine. "Gentlemen, tonight isn't an ending—it's a beginning. The future favors the bold. We will not be small."

Smiles around the table; murmurs of agreement. Charles raised his glass with the rest, luck warming his chest. Michael smiled too, but with his eyes narrowed—measuring the cost of boldness.

# CHAPTER 15

The bell above the coffee shop door jingled as Camilla stepped into a pocket of warm air scented with espresso and sugar. Shadows stretched long across the polished floor; afternoon light slipped through slatted blinds in noirish bars of gold and gray. She paused the memory of her mothers face —one heartbeat too long—and the room tilted.

The world swam. The counter blurred.

Johnny's arms caught her again before she could fall, steady and sure.

"Hey—easy. I've got you."

He smiled, his voice low and teasing. "Didn't I tell you, needed that cup of coffee right?"

When her vision cleared, she found herself staring once more into Johnny's face—handsome, yes, but it was his eyes that held her. There was something disarming there, a warmth that felt both kind and dangerously perceptive. For a breathless moment, the rest of the café dissolved around them.

He guided her gently into a chair and crouched to her level. "Breathe with me," he murmured. "In... out. That's it."

Her pulse slowed. She let out a shaky laugh. "Apparently, my dignity enjoys fainting in public. I can't believe that happened again. I really need to eat breakfast before I go out."

"Dignity's overrated," he said, pressing a glass of water into her hands. "Here—sip. Sugar helps. Want a croissant? Three?"

"One," she whispered, and his smile widened.

They sat together, cappuccinos between them, the foam in hers swirled like a galaxy. Their talk stretched—her voice halting at first, his patient. He told her he painted, mostly people. Faces. "The parts they don't realize they're showing," he said, and grinned when she called it invasive.

He had a way of paying attention that felt almost too much, like he was seeing more than she meant to reveal.

Finally, as the conversation softened into ease, she leaned back. "So your name is Johnny?"

He repeated it "Yes, Johnny."

He chuckled feeling more comfortable with her too and thinking his cute story would amuse her "My mother wanted it spelled with two i's. Johnnii. Said it looked more... alive." His lashes dipped as he smiled at the memory. "Not that I use it much. Except for legal paperwork. And free pastries."

Her heart pounded. *Johnnii.* The name she and her mother had given her violin—their secret.

"I—" She stood abruptly. "I have to go."

"Did I say something wrong?"

"No. You've been very kind. I just remembered something." She grabbed her purse, almost left it, then clutched it like a shield. "Thank you. For everything."

Before he could reply, she fled.

The bell above the door jingled as she vanished.

From the side entrance, a lanky man strolled in with a guitar case over his shoulder. "So that's why you were late," he teased, nudging Johnny. "Catching clumsy girls? I should be worried about competition."

Johnny kept his gaze on the door. "She simply slipped. I gave her water. And pastry diplomacy."

Joey smirked at the cappuccinos. "Two cups. Bold. Did you at least get her name?"

"Yeah," Johnny murmured. "She got mine and ran."

Joey laughed. "Classic. Come on, we've got to load in the equipment at the club, take a couple of hours. You coming?"

Johnny sighed, but his smile lingered faintly as he picked up his sketchbook. "Yeah. Let's go be useful."

Camilla stormed into her house like a storm cloud breaking. Paola called from the kitchen, "I made supper—are you hungry?"

But Camilla was already halfway up the stairs. In her room she slammed the door, her purse and coat crashing onto the bed.

"What just happened?" she whispered. "Johnny is a common name, but two i's? Only my mother and I knew."

Her thoughts tangled, anger and longing fighting in her chest. "Why am I so distrusting? He was kind, and I—" She broke off, tears hot and sudden.

"Camilla?" Her father's voice rang from the hall. "I am home. Decided to have supper with you. Are you up there?"

She forced her voice steady. "Yes, Father! I'll be right down."

Powder, cold water, a quick mask of composure. Then she joined him in the dining room, where Charles sat glowing with triumph.

"Everything go as planned today?" he asked carefully. "With the little problem we discussed this morning?"

"Yes, Father, all is fine." She smiled too quickly. "And how was your day?"

That was all the cue he needed. He launched into his story—Raptnor's authority, the merger's swiftness, his own clever remarks at the table. He embellished until the air itself seemed gilded. "and to make it even more exciting we are meeting for another elegant dinner to lay out the steps of the merger – do you believe this not a cold banks office but a high class establishment – that's how I want to run my business Camilla do you get it?" with a big smile on his face clearly in his own world.

Camilla nodded when she had to, then spun her own lie: nails, library, the violin. "Mr. Hempshaw was pleased with the gift," she said flatly. "He'll appraise it. I'll get a fair price."

"Well, great, honey," Charles said, lifting his glass. "Sounds like you had a fine day."

They ate in silence, beneath chandeliers and polished crystal, both wearing masks, both keeping secrets.

Charles deep in thought about his success and soaring career.

Camilla deep in thought about Johnny and softening, she ran out of the coffee shop so fast she didn't even give him a chance.

# CHAPTER 16

The stairwell creaked as Camilla stepped onto it, her hand brushing the cold railing. It was wrought iron, old but elaborate, the kind of craftsmanship from another century. The metal twisted and curled in ornate patterns of leaves and vines, each curve catching the dim light from a single hanging bulb above.

The staircase wound upward in a slow spiral, its iron spine groaning faintly under her weight. Dusty sunlight filtered through a tall window on the landing, striping the steps in gold. The echo of her shoes rang against the iron, a hollow, haunting sound that carried both warning and invitation.

It was not grand like her father's marble staircase, but it had a soul. Every groove in the worn steps, every curve in the carved metal, felt alive with the weight of years. As she climbed, Camilla felt as though she were crossing into another realm—away from the rigid order of her world and toward something unknown, colorful, and free.

At the top, Johnny pushed open the loft door, and warmth and light spilled out, a shock after the cool shadows of the stairwell.

Camilla stepped inside—and stopped.

The loft was nothing like she expected.

Yes, canvases leaned against the walls, brushes filled chipped mugs, and sketches sprawled across every surface—but this was not the chaotic workshop she had imagined. It was a home, vibrant and alive.

Bright flowers crowded the windowsills, splashes of red, yellow, and violet reaching eagerly toward the light. A soft, overstuffed couch sat draped with patchwork throws, its cushions slouching invitingly. Next to it, a giant bean bag chair rested like a waiting companion. In the center, an old wooden chest served as a coffee table, its surface stacked with sketchbooks and a bowl of tangerines.

The floorboards glowed honey-gold beneath scattered rugs woven in bold, mismatched patterns. An emerald velvet armchair sat tucked by the window, its back worn smoothly from use, and a crooked lamp painted in streaks of orange and teal stood proudly beside it.

The walls were alive with art: finished canvases, half-finished studies, sketches tacked at odd angles, every surface humming with color and imagination. Yet the room was neat, cared for. The wildness was deliberate, like a symphony of details arranged by a conductor.

It smelled of flowers and paint, with just a whisper of coffee—a comforting blend that wrapped around her like an embrace.

Above the fireplace hung a single framed portrait that commanded the room: an old man with a lined face, silver hair, and eyes startlingly young and alive. They followed her, kind and knowing, and she felt immediately as if he could see more of her than she wanted revealed.

"You like my place?" Johnny asked, watching her take it in.

"Yes, I do," Camilla said honestly. "It's as if there's life everywhere you turn."

He laughed. "I collected everything myself. Decorated, if you can call it that. I'm a bachelor, but I need color. Makes it easier to come home."

"Well, I am impressed."

He gestured to the loveseat. "Sit. I'll make coffee. Though, dare I risk repeating last time?"

She laughed softly. "I suppose I owe you an explanation about that."

"Then coffee it is." He ground beans, poured water, and returned with two steaming cups. Sitting beside her, he leaned in just enough to unsettle her composure. "All right, strange, beautiful girl. Why did you run?"

She hesitated, fingers circling the rim of her cup. "You're making fun of me."

"No, I'm not. Now—talk first, or coffee first?"

"Coffee first," she said, buying time.

They sipped in silence. Finally, she sighed. "It was your name. That's why I bolted."

"My name?"

"Yes. Johnny. A common enough name—but not the way you spell it. With two i's." Her voice trembled. "No one spells it that way. Except my mother and me."

Johnny blinked. "My mother wanted it that way, yes, but my father wouldn't allow it on official papers. I'm just plain Johnny. Camilla... what does my name have to do with anything?"

She closed her eyes, and the room slipped away. Music swelled in her memory, sunlight flickered through trees, and she was a child again in her mother's secret garden.

**FLASHBACK**

"When I was little," she began softly, "my mother and I had a secret world. My father wanted order, money, high society. My mother wanted music, freedom, dance. She gave up everything for him—her family, her heritage—except her dancing. That she couldn't let go.

"When Father was gone and the staff distracted, we would sneak into the garden. She had hidden bright skirts and ribbons in the back of his closet, away from his navy suits. She would dress herself in color, crown me with flowers, and set up a phonograph under the bushes. There, she danced just for me—skirts flying, bracelets clattering, long black hair tossing as she twirled. She was Gypsy Fire. And I was her audience."

Camilla's voice thickened with memory. "One day, the phonograph was ruined by rain. She wouldn't be stopped. She brought out a violin—an heirloom from her family. She said she thought I had music in me. I was so small, but I begged her to let me play. 'Mommy, I can be your music,' I told her."

Her throat caught. "She showed me how to hold it, how to bow a simple Gypsy melody. Somehow it wasn't heavy anymore. It was as if it wanted to play. And from then on, she danced, and I played. We were inseparable."

Camilla's hands clenched in her lap. "One day I asked her the violin's name. She told me it once belonged to Janos Borza, a great Gypsy violinist. I couldn't pronounce it. I stammered and finally blurted out, 'Johnny.' She laughed—and said if I wanted it to be special, we'd spell it with two i's. J-o-h-n-n-i-i."

Her eyes shone. "It was our secret. Our name. My violin was Johnnii. No one else knew. So when you told me yours..." She shook her head. "I thought you were mocking me, or that somehow you knew. I panicked."

The silence stretched. Johnny looked at her, not with mockery, but with soft astonishment.

"I see," he said at last. "That must have been... overwhelming. But Camilla—it's a coincidence. Strange, yes, but not cruel."

Before she could answer, he rose quickly. "Wait here."

He disappeared upstairs, then returned carrying a case. He set it on the table, opened it slowly, and revealed the violin—restored, gleaming, its scars mended, its strings waiting.

Camilla gasped. "You have it! Mr. Hempshaw told me he appraised it and had a buyer" She reached for her checkbook. "Please, let me buy it back."

Johnny gently pushed her hand away. "It can't be bought. But you can earn it back. Two conditions."

Her eyes narrowed. "What conditions?"

"First—you must play it. Only you can tell if I restored it properly. Second—" His eyes sparkled. "Let me paint you."

She laughed nervously. "With or without clothes?"

"With," he teased, then lowered his lashes. "Unless you prefer otherwise."

Her laughter rang brightly, easing the weight of her past memory.

She lifted the violin, its wood warm against her skin. For a moment it was heavy, awkward. Then Johnny's hand covered hers, guiding the bow. And in that instant, she felt her mother's hands too—superimposed, whispering in her ear:

*Let the music open your heart.*

She drew the bow. The first notes wavered, then steadied. The loft shimmered with sound. The flowers on the sill seemed to sway, the portrait's painted eyes seemed to brighten, and Johnny painted furiously, trying to capture the unseen glow that surrounded her.

When the last note faded, silence held them both.

"You're a natural," Johnny said softly. "Bravo."

Camilla bowed playfully, and in the corner of her vision, she thought she saw her mother's figure bowing, too, with a smile.

"You can keep it here," Johnny added, taking the violin gently from her hands. "Safe. Play whenever you come to pose."

Surprised at his intuition "How did you know I was afraid to bring it back home...my father..."

"I know you, don't try and figure out why I just do" Johnny said confidently

Her relief was overwhelming. "Thank you. Truly."

She reached for her coat and started walking out the door but Johnny stopped her.  "Don't go yet, the evening is young, please stay awhile"

He moved in closer to her, a breath away, silent, their bodies close.

They didn't move right away. Instead, Johnny touched her hand, tentative but sure. She leaned into him without thinking, and he drew her closer.

What began as a simple embrace stretched into stillness. Time slipped away unnoticed. They lay curled together on the soft couch, his heartbeat steady beneath her ear, the patchwork throws warming them, the faint scent of paint and flowers drifting through the quiet.

Neither spoke. Words would have broken the spell. The sun sank across the windows, shadows lengthening, until the loft glowed with the dusky light of evening.

At last, Camilla stirred. "I should go," she whispered.

Johnny's arms tightened once before letting her go. He smiled, eyes luminous in the fading light. "Tomorrow, then."

She nodded, gathered her things, and stepped toward the door, heart aching with both comfort and longing.

Just as she crossed the threshold, she thought she heard the faintest trace of violin music—one lingering phrase, tender and insistent.

Her mother's voice followed, soft as breath:

*Let the music open your heart.*

# CHAPTER 17

Crystal light spilled from the chandeliers of the private dining hall, scattering brilliance across cut-glass decanters and polished silver domes. Waiters glided between the tables—silent, precise, their movements as choreographed as the evening itself.

Charles sat stiff-backed at the long mahogany table, every gesture measured, every word carefully weighed. Tonight was Raptnor's show—there was no mistaking that—but Charles allowed himself to bask in the reflected glow. The merger had gone through with astonishing speed, far faster than he'd dared to hope. For him, it meant access to the inner circle he had long coveted, a foot on the first rung of a higher ladder.

Down the table, assistants and secretaries lined the far side like dutiful soldiers, stacks of folders and notepads at the ready, poised to capture every directive that fell from their employers' lips.

Raptnor presided over it all with a predator's ease—smiling, charming, utterly in control. While others worked, he dined lavishly, savoring wine and rare delicacies, surrounded by his closest executives. Among them now sat Charles and Michael, invited at last to feast at the same table.

# CHAPTER 18

That same evening, Camilla slipped quietly into the house, her steps soft on the marble floor. She carried with her the warmth of the loft—the smell of flowers, the hum of the violin, the feel of Johnny's arms around her. Hours had vanished there, curled together in a world of color and sound so unlike the cold brilliance of this one.

The mansion was silent, its chandeliers extinguished, its polished surfaces reflecting only emptiness. Camilla climbed the staircase alone, her fingers trailing along the smooth banister. In her room, she pressed her hand to her heart, as though to hold onto the glow before it faded.

Outside her window, the last light of day lingered. In the hush of twilight, she thought she heard it again—the faint, haunting echo of a violin phrase.

And with it, her mother's voice, soft as breath, certain as truth:

*Let the music open your heart.*

# CHAPTER 19

The next day, Camilla found herself climbing the winding iron stairwell once more, the elaborate curves of its railing now less foreboding, more like a secret path into another life. The heavy quiet of her father's house still clung to her, but as soon as Johnny opened the loft door, light and color spilled over her like an embrace.

"You came back," he said, his smile quick and warm. His large brown eyes caught the sunlight, lashes casting shadows on his cheek.

"I said I would," she answered, her voice softer than she intended.

The violin case waited on the old chest, its polished surface gleaming as though it had been waiting just for her. But Johnny was already setting up an easel near the window, canvas blank and eager.

"I told you there were two conditions," he said, his tone light. "You've fulfilled the first. Now we begin the second."

"You mean I have to sit still for hours while you stare at me?" Camilla teased, lowering herself into the chair he pointed out.

He grinned. "Precisely. Try not to enjoy it too much."

She tilted her head. And asked again still testing him

"With or without clothes?"

"With," he said smoothly, then leaned in closer, his voice dropping to a playful whisper. "Unless you insist otherwise."

She laughed, her tension easing, and folded her hands in her lap.

Johnny began to sketch, charcoal moving quick and sure across the canvas. His gaze flicked between her face and the paper, not in the way of a man appraising beauty, but of an artist searching for something beneath the surface. His eyes seemed to look through her, seeing not just the lines of her cheek and jaw but the tremors of thought, the rhythm of her breath.

The room was quiet except for the scratch of charcoal and the occasional creak of the floorboards as she shifted. Time slowed again. She realized with a start that she liked the silence with him, the way it wasn't empty but full of unspoken things.

At last, Johnny set down the charcoal. "There," he said, turning the canvas slightly—but just enough to block her view.

She leaned forward. "Let me see!"

He shook his head, smiling. "An artist never reveals a painting until it's finished. Magic hates spoilers."

"Impossible," she muttered, sinking back into the chair.

"Guilty," he replied.

She sighed, glancing at the violin on the chest. "Then may I at least play?"

Johnny nodded. "Always."


She lifted the instrument, nestling it into the curve of her shoulder. This time it was easier, the weight less daunting. As the first notes rose, her body swayed with the rhythm. The loft filled again with sound, the light deepening around her.

Johnny sat back, sketch forgotten, watching as if the music itself painted something on the air.

And in the corner of her eye, Camilla glimpsed her mother's spirit again, radiant and calm, whispering:

*Let the music open your heart.*

The bow stilled. Silence followed, thick and alive.

Johnny leaned forward, his voice quiet but certain. "Camilla, you belong to this. Don't let anyone tell you otherwise."

She lowered her gaze, thinking of her father's face, of his dismissive words. But here, in this loft, with flowers blooming on the sills and color spilling from every wall, the weight of her world lifted.

...For now, at least, she was free.

Just then, the door burst open without so much as a knock.

"Johnny, you in here? I swear, if you ditched me with the amps again—"

A tall, lanky young man stumbled in, hair sticking out in wild tufts, a guitar case slung carelessly over his shoulder. He froze when he saw Camilla, his eyes widening.

"Well, hello," he said, flashing a grin. "Didn't know you had company. Should I bow, or...?" He bent into a ridiculous stage bow, nearly dropping the guitar.

Camilla stifled a laugh, startled but amused.

"Joey," Johnny groaned, running a hand over his face. "This is Camilla. Camilla, this is Joey—musician, roadie, professional nuisance.""Hey, I'll take that as a compliment," Joey said, plopping the guitar case onto the bean bag chair. "So, this is the mysterious muse you've been going on about?"

Johnny shot him a look sharp enough to cut, but Joey only grinned wider. "Don't mind him," Johnny said quickly, turning back to Camilla. "He talks too much."

"I prefer to call it... artistic enthusiasm," Joey quipped, then winked at Camilla. "And I can tell already, you've got patience. That'll come in handy, trust me."

"Out," Johnny ordered, though his eyes betrayed amusement.

Joey held up his hands in surrender. "Fine, fine. I'll be downstairs. But don't forget, gig's at nine. And bring your muse if she wants a night out."

He disappeared down the stairwell, humming loudly, his off-key notes trailing behind him.

Camilla shook her head, smiling despite herself. "Your friends are... lively."

Johnny chuckled, stepping closer, his big brown eyes catching the last of the sunset light. "That's one word for it."

The moment softened again, the air charged between them. He reached for her hand, brushing his thumb lightly across her knuckles.

"You should go before it gets too late," he said gently, though his tone betrayed reluctance.

She nodded, but neither of them moved.

"Tomorrow?" he asked. "Yes... tomorrow."

She turned toward the door, but Johnny caught her wrist, pulling her back just enough that she stumbled lightly against him. His grin was crooked, playful.

"You can't leave without a proper goodnight," he murmured.

Before she could answer, his lips met hers—soft at first, testing, then deepening with warmth and a teasing sweetness that made her laugh against his mouth. He drew back only when she was breathless, still caught between laughter and something more.

"That's better," he said with mock seriousness. "Now you may go."

Camilla pressed her hand to a flushed cheek, smiling as she slipped through the door.

On the stairwell, her heart still racing, she thought she heard it again—the faint echo of violin strings, like a blessing following her into the night.

Her mother's voice trailed after it, tender and sure:

*Let the music open your heart.*

# CHAPTER 20

The long dining table gleamed under crystal light, though only one place was set. Charles sat at its head, swirling the last sip of his brandy, his mind replaying every detail of the Raptnor evening. The deal was sealed, the door to power swung open, and already his imagination roared with expansion.

But beneath his triumph, a small unease gnawed at him. Michael Smithers' silence still troubled him. The man had looked at him oddly, almost pityingly, when the contracts were signed. Charles pushed the thought away — Smithers had always been a worrier. The important thing was the green light. Raptnor's green light.

The front door opened, footsteps soft against marble.

"Camilla?"

She appeared at the threshold of the dining room, cheeks flushed, eyes bright. For a moment, Charles studied her as if seeing her for the first time. She was radiant, though not in the polished way he preferred. No expensive gown, no jewelry — yet something glowed in her, something he couldn't name.

"You're late," he said finally.

"Sorry, Father." Her voice was even, but her fingers twisted nervously in her coat.

Charles tilted his head, narrowing his eyes. "Where have you been?"

"The library," she said smoothly. "Working on my research paper."

He let the lie pass — for now. But he noticed the flush in her cheeks, the lightness in her step, the way she seemed... softened. Different. Happier. Almost glowing.

"You seem... changed," he said at last.

Camilla froze. "Changed?"

"Yes. Happier. I suppose that's good." His tone was flat, but suspicion coiled beneath it. "Still, remember who you are, Camilla. Appearances matter. One must never be careless."

Her smile was brittle. "Yes, Father."

She excused herself quickly, retreating upstairs. In her room, she shut the door, heart racing. She ached for the violin—but it was safe, hidden at Johnny's loft, waiting for her return. That was the only way she could keep her father from discovering it.

She pressed her hand against her chest, trying to hold onto the memory of the music, of Johnny's arms, of her mother's whisper that still echoed faintly in her ear:

*Let the music open your heart.*

Downstairs, Charles swirled the dregs of his brandy, his unease sharpening. Something had shifted in his daughter, and he intended to find out what it was.

# CHAPTER 21

Julie Warrington had been Camilla's neighbor and best friend since childhood. After her mother's death, Camilla spent more and more time at the Warringtons' house, often considering them a second family.

Julie was a tall, statuesque blonde with sparkling blue eyes and a smile that could light up a room. Despite her natural beauty, she never flaunted it—usually pulling her long hair into a clip, swiping on just enough makeup to pass, and covering her curves with baggy jeans and oversized T-shirts. It drove her mother crazy, but Julie never seemed to care.

Unlike Charles, who corrected Camilla constantly, the Warringtons encouraged Julie to be herself. They never silenced her, never demanded she become someone she wasn't. Camilla admired that freedom, sometimes even envied it.

The Warrington women came from a long line of trailblazers: Julie's grandmother had been one of the first recognized female surgeons in the country, her mother a respected cardiologist, and her sister fresh from medical school. It was assumed Julie would follow suit, but she quickly discovered that the sight of blood made her faint. Instead, she found her passion in words and truth. Investigative reporting called to her like nothing else, and once Julie caught the scent of a story, she was relentless—like a dog with a bone.

Her family never excluded her for choosing a different path. They supported her unconditionally, which only deepened Camilla's longing for that kind of acceptance. Charles, however, frowned on Julie's influence, calling her "too free-spirited." He tolerated her only because she came from the right kind of family stock, and he liked the polish of her family name.

Camilla, of course, adored her. Julie was her anchor, her truth-teller, and her constant. The ringtone she had assigned her friend—*"You Don't Own Me"*—fit her perfectly.

Julie hadn't seen much of Camilla lately and decided it was time to find out what was going on. She arrived at the front steps of Camilla's house just in time to see her friend flying out the door and nearly running right past her.

"Hey!" Julie shouted. "What the hell? Has it been that long you don't remember me?"

Camilla stopped short, guilt flashing across her face. "I'm so sorry, Julie. I'm running late for an appointment and didn't even notice you."

Julie crossed her arms. "Uh-huh. And where exactly are you running off to?"

"The... library," Camilla stammered. "I have some studying to do."

Julie arched an eyebrow. "Really? Since when do you make appointments with the library? And besides, who goes to the library anymore?"

"I do. I like the quiet," Camilla replied quickly. "Please, can we talk later?"

Julie shook her head, her tone sharp. "Nope. Guess what—you're going to be late for your *'library appointment'* because we're having coffee first. You've been dodging me, not answering calls, ignoring texts. We're talking. Now."

Knowing resistance was useless, Camilla sighed. "Fine. Coffee first. Library second."

They ended up at the corner coffeehouse—Johnny's coffeehouse. The sight of their usual corner table made Camilla's stomach twist, and she kept darting glances toward it, half-afraid he might appear.

Julie leaned across the table. "All right, girl. Spill. What's going on with you?"

Camilla tried casually. "Nothing. Just busy with schoolwork"

"Don't even try," Julie interrupted. "You only fiddle with your purse strap when you're hiding something. So, talk."

Camilla hesitated, then gave in. "Okay... I've been busy, and it's something my father would not approve of. That's why I've been quiet—even with you. I'm sorry, Jules."

Julie's eyes lit up. "Ooooh. Something Daddy wouldn't like? Let me guess—you're moonlighting as a waitress at a truck stop? Or better—" she smirked, "—you fell for a trucker while you were on your shift."

Camilla burst out laughing. "No! Not a trucker."

"Then it's a man. I knew it!" Julie leaned in eagerly. "Tell me everything. Muscles? Nice buns? Please say he has nice buns."

Camilla shook her head, tears of laughter in her eyes. "You are impossible."

"Guilty." Julie grinned. "So what's the story?"

Camilla sobered. "I met someone. His name is Johnny. He's... not at all the kind of man my father would accept. He repaired my violin. He—he's an artist. He's painting my portrait."

Julie's eyes widened. "Oh my God. That is so European romance novel of you. The mysterious handsome painter in his loft above the music shop. I love it. Are you posing nude?"

Camilla groaned. "No! He's serious about his art."

"So no hanky-panky yet?"

Camilla avoided her gaze. "We just met."

Julie narrowed her eyes. "Uh-huh. And yet you're glowing like a lantern. Cammy, I've never seen you like this."

Camilla exhaled and finally let it pour out: her connection with Johnny, the way she felt comfortable with him, how different it was from the constant facade she wore for her father. "With Johnny, I can just... be myself. Do you know how rare that is? It scares me. But it feels so natural. Like breathing."

Julie softened, reaching across the table. "Hey. It's okay. You know I'll support you no matter what. Your secret's safe with me."

Camilla's eyes shone. "Thank you, Jules. I love you."

"I love you too. But listen—be careful, okay? Maybe this is real. Maybe it's just an escape. Just don't lose yourself."

Camilla hugged her tightly. "The only way not to get hurt is not to live. And I refuse to live that way."

Julie smiled, shaking her head. "Fine, Shakespeare. Go see your bohemian boyfriend in his secret artist's lair." She twirled an imaginary mustache. "Better to have loved and lost, eh?"

Camilla laughed, grabbing her purse. "You're ridiculous."

"Ridiculously right," Julie shot back. "Now go. Before your 'library appointment' gets cranky."

# CHAPTER 22

Camilla's heart still raced from her talk with Julie as she climbed the winding iron stairwell, each ornate curve of the railing catching the afternoon light. Julie's teasing still echoed in her mind—*the bohemian boyfriend in his artist's lair*—but as she reached the top landing, the joke dissolved into reality.

Johnny was waiting.

He pulled the door open before she knocked, as though he'd been standing there, listening for her footsteps. "I thought you might not come," he said softly.

"I almost didn't," she admitted, her voice catching. "But here I am."

His smile was slow, disarming. "Then let's begin."

The loft was bathed in amber glow, sunlight falling across the easel where a fresh canvas stretched, blank and expectant. Johnny gestured to the chair he'd set near the window.

"Sit, please. Look toward the light. Perfect."

Camilla perched on the chair, her hands folded, trying to appear calm. She felt his gaze on her—not invasive, not possessive, but searching, as if he were trying to find something beneath her skin. His charcoal moved quickly, lines racing across the canvas.

"You know," she said, forcing a smile, "it's unnerving being stared at like this."

Johnny chuckled. "Don't think of it as staring. Think of it as… listening, but with my eyes."

"That's worse!" she laughed, shaking her head. She tilted her head slightly trying to get a secret peek at the painting, but to no avail Johnny kept it well concealed.

He grinned, but kept on painting his hand never stopping. "An artist never shows the painting until it's finished. Remember?"

Camilla sighed. "Still feels unfair."

"You'll thank me later."

The scratch of charcoal filled the room, steady and rhythmic, until at last he set it down. "That's enough for today. Rest your face before it forgets how to smile."

She leaned back in the chair, relieved, and her gaze drifted toward the old chest where her violin case gleamed. Johnny followed her eyes.

"Go on," he said. "He's waiting for you."

Camilla lifted the violin, nestling it against her shoulder. As she drew the bow across the strings, a soft, haunting melody rose—hesitant at first, then swelling with confidence. And with it came her mother's presence again, brighter, closer.

Johnny sat quietly, his eyes half-closed, as though the music painted him as much as he painted her.

The air between them thickened, and before she could step back, Johnny bent and brushed his lips against hers—gentle, lingering, filled with a warmth that made her chest ache.

Camilla leaned into the kiss, her free hand resting against his shoulder, the violin still cradled between them. For a moment, time unraveled—the world outside gone, her father's rules forgotten, Julie's warnings distant. There was only this: the kiss, the music, the echo of her mother's voice.

*Let the music open your heart.*

# CHAPTER 23

Charles sat behind his heavy mahogany desk, the morning papers spread across its polished surface. Reports of mergers and acquisitions dominated the headlines, but his eyes kept drifting back to the clock.

Camilla had been gone often these past weeks. Excuses about the library. Study groups. Research. He told himself she was a dutiful daughter, yet something in her tone gnawed at him. She seemed brighter, yes—but with a secret kind of brightness, the kind that hid rather than revealed.

And Charles distrusted secrets.

He picked up the phone, dialing without hesitation. "Michael," he said when Smithers' voice answered, "we'll need to go over the finer points of the Raptnor contract again. Lunch. Tomorrow. Same club."

Smithers hesitated. "Of course, Charles. But—"

"No buts." Charles cut him off. He was not about to let even Smithers' quiet doubts shake his triumph.

After the call, Charles leaned back in his chair, fingers steepled. His triumph with Raptnor was only half satisfying if his own household felt unsettled. He had built his life on control, precision, appearances. And now his daughter was slipping beyond his reach.

That evening, as Camilla floated in with a distracted smile, he watched her more carefully than ever.

"You were at the library again?" he asked casually over dinner.

"Yes," she said smoothly. "Research."

"For what class?"

Camilla froze just a fraction of a second too long. "European history."

Charles nodded, filing the pause away in the ledger of his mind. "Good. Education is everything."

They ate in silence for a time, the clink of silverware loud against porcelain. At last, he said, "I've noticed you're spending quite a lot of time away. Perhaps I'll have Paola drive you to your appointments. Safer that way."

Her fork slipped, nearly clattering to the plate. "That won't be necessary, Father. Really, I'm fine."

Charles smiled thinly, hiding his satisfaction. Her reaction told him everything: she was hiding something.

"Very well," he said smoothly. "But don't think I won't notice. Remember, Camilla—appearances matter."

She nodded, forcing a polite smile. But upstairs, behind her closed door, her heart hammered. Her world with Johnny had to remain hidden. If her father ever found out, everything—Johnny, the violin, the portrait, her freedom—would vanish.

And Charles, sipping his brandy downstairs, vowed silently: he would discover her secret.

# CHAPTER 24

The loft was quiet except for the sound of brushes clinking in a glass jar. Camilla shifted uneasily on the loveseat, sensing Johnny's eyes on her. His hand hovered near his palette, but his expression was far away, as though weighing something unsaid.

Deciding the best strategy was to change the subject, Johnny suddenly brightened. "Hey, I have something for you today. Something for the portrait."

Camilla tilted her head, curious. "Oh? What is it?"

"It's a surprise." His grin was playful, but his eyes were serious. He guided her gently back onto the loveseat, arranging her arms and legs to match the pose from their last sitting. "Now close your eyes."

She obeyed without hesitation. "All right."

She waited, her heart thudding, until something soft brushed against her neck. Silky, velvet, cool at first—then warming as Johnny smoothed it over her chest. His fingertips grazed her collarbone, making her breath catch.

"Don't open your eyes," he whispered. "Tell me what you feel."

A smile tugged at her lips. She loved his strange little games. "Okay... silky, satiny material."

"Not the texture. The feeling. What does it stir in you?"

She hesitated. "Warmth. Comfort. But more than that..." Her voice softened. "I feel beauty. I don't even know what beauty feels like, but that's the only word that fits. Beauty—and music."

Opening her eyes, she gasped. Draped across her shoulders was a multicolored scarf, its colors vibrant as a Gypsy's skirts. It was startlingly similar to the scarves her mother used to wear.

"Oh, Johnny—it's beautiful! Where did you find it?"

He sidestepped the question. "I want you to wear it for the portrait. You need color—something that reflects who you are. This felt right."

Camilla reached for the edge, ready to adjust it. "At least give me a mirror, so I can put it on straighter."

"Don't move." His voice was firm now. "It's perfect. Stay exactly as you are."

His brush flew across the canvas, faster and with more intensity than she had ever seen. He worked like a man possessed, mixing colors, sweeping strokes, stepping back, then lunging forward again, his gaze darting between her face and the scarf.

At last, he lowered his brush, chest rising with exertion. "That's it. That's what I wanted. You finally came out."

"What do you mean? Can I see?"

"No." He covered the canvas with a cloth before she could rise. "It's not finished, and an artist.." Camilla finished his sentence "...never shows his work unfinished." "I know, I know"

She pouted, half teasing, half disappointed. "You're impossible. Now I can't wait until next time."

"Patience, Camilla. Art demands it." His eyes, however, sparkled with satisfaction.

She reached for her coat, but Johnny caught her wrist. "Must you leave so soon?" His thumb brushed lightly against her pulse, his voice dropping. "Stay."

Her cheeks warmed, her breath hitching—until he stepped back suddenly, retrieving her violin from behind the easel. He held it out reverently. "Play something for me. Your music... it moves me more than anything."

Camilla took the instrument, the polished wood alive under her fingertips. The bow touched the strings, and a melody poured out—hesitant at first, then swelling with confidence, as though her mother herself guided her hands. She heard another subtle message her mothers whisper.

*Let the dance set you free*

When the final note trembled into silence, Johnny set the violin aside and reached for her waist. "Now dance with me."

She laughed in protest, but he spun her anyway. The scarf fluttered as they moved, the colors alive in the air. Their steps grew wilder, laughter echoing against brick walls, until they collapsed breathless onto the couch.

His lips brushed her temple, her cheek, the corner of her mouth—playful yet tender, each kiss sending shivers down her spine. She melted into his arms, her back pressed to his chest, his arm wrapped protectively around her waist.

Their laughter faded, replaced by the slow rhythm of shared breath. As her eyelids drooped, Camilla thought she heard the faintest echo of a violin in the air, and her mother's voice, gentle as ever:

*Let the music open your heart, let the dance set you free*

# CHAPTER 25

Charles tossed and turned in his large, comfortable bed, then finally gave up. Staring at the ceiling only deepened the pit in his stomach. Lately, he'd had more bad days than good ones—constant arguments with Camilla, a daughter slipping further out of his control, and the gnawing sense that something was not right at the bank.

He slid into his slippers, stretched, yawned, and wandered to the window. Outside, the sky was a flat gray curtain, the drizzle tapping against the glass. "Rain on top of everything else..." he muttered.

A quick shower, a bagel, and a coffee later, he settled into the back seat of his limousine. Even the city looked different today—subdued, tense.

When the car pulled up to the bank, silence hung heavier than usual. Too quiet. Too still. Something was wrong.

Inside, his secretary Sylvia hurried toward him, her expression strained. Not the bright smile he counted on to start his mornings, but a pale, nervous glance.

"Sir... there are men waiting in your office. I tried to have them sit here in the lobby, but they insisted."

"Men?" Charles frowned.

Her voice dropped. "Sir, they have badges."

He froze. "What?"

Forcing composure, Charles straightened his tie, smoothed his jacket, and strode toward his office. He could not afford to look shaken.

The sight that greeted him chilled him to the bone: three men in gray suits. Everything about them seemed drained of color—gray hair, gray eyes, gray expressions. The one in the center spoke first.

"Are you Charles Huntington?" His voice was flat, mechanical.

"Yes," Charles replied evenly. "And you are?"

The man flipped open a badge with a snap. "FBI. Agent Brown. These are Agents Mack and Jerod. We have a few questions for you."

Charles' throat tightened, but he forced a smooth reply. "About what, may I ask?"

"About one of your account holders. Mr. Sergio Joaquin Morelia."

Charles blinked, stalling. "We have thousands of accounts, Agent. I don't know them all personally."

"Really." Agent Brown's eyes narrowed. "So you're saying you did not open an account for Mr. Morelia? That he does not have ties to this bank?" His tone carried an edge of sarcasm.

"I said no such thing," Charles countered. "Only that I don't know the details of every client."

Brown slipped a paper from his jacket. "This is a court order authorizing us to examine all bank records. Agents Mack and Jerod will begin immediately."

Charles' composure cracked. "Excuse me, I'll need to call my attorney." He stepped into the doorway, raising his voice. "Sylvia! Get Miles on the phone. Now."

"Yes, sir," Sylvia stammered.

 

Back in his office, Charles lowered himself into his chair, hands gripping the armrests. The gray men were already spreading out, briefcases opening, files stacking, pens scratching. His world—his empire—was no longer his alone.

The pit in his stomach grew heavier. For the first time in decades, Charles Huntington was not in control.

# CHAPTER 26

Charles had convinced himself that things were finally returning to order. His daughter was dressing conservatively, her shopping reflected restraint, and more than once she had told him she was going to the club for tennis or buried in business textbooks at the library. He took pride in her sudden interest in his kind of pursuits—finance, discipline, propriety.

Yes, he thought, she was learning. She was finally coming around.

But beneath the polished surface, cracks widened. The merger had already gone through, and instead of the clean triumph he had imagined, it had brought only scrutiny. Federal agents were now a constant shadow—questions, subpoenas, whispers in the corridors. Every morning, he entered his office with the same gnawing dread: what would they uncover today?

Still, he clung to Camilla's apparent compliance as a lifeline. If business was under siege, at least his household seemed steady. He had ridden the house of the violin, that constant wedge between them, though Camilla still managed to keep a subscription or two to music and dance magazines. He chose to overlook them, sure that they, too, would soon fade away.

At least, he hoped.

Upstairs, Camilla heard the faint creak of the mail slot and flew down the staircase two at a time. She had been waiting for something— something important.

Her heart sank when she found her father already holding a magazine, her name on the label. She watched in horror as he began to rip it in half.

"Hey! That's addressed to me!"

"Oh, this?" Charles said casually. "Since you've decided to give up the violin, I thought you didn't need these anymore. Just more junk mail." He tore it into quarters, his movements brisk, dismissive.

"No!" She lunged forward, grabbing for the pieces. "That is not your decision to make. It's mine."

Her father continued, his jaw tight, shredding the paper into confetti. The cover—*The Gypsy Serenade Newsletter*—tore down the middle, scattering across the marble floor. He tossed the fragments into the air like so much debris, then stormed into the den and slammed the door.

Camilla dropped to her knees, gathering each scrap as if they were pieces of her own heart. Cradling them in her hands, she whispered, "It's not over, is it? He didn't get his way... and neither did I."

The sight of the torn pages on her white bedspread pulled her backward into memory.

She was ten years old again, kneeling by her bed after prayers when her father entered, his face carved with stone.

"Your mother is gone, Camilla. She died today."

Her small voice trembled. "What? Where is Mommy?"

"Heaven," he said mechanically, as if trying the word on his tongue. He put stiff arms around her, not for comfort but for duty, before turning away. "It is just the two of us now. We will get on with our life."

He left her sobbing in the shadows.

Clutching her violin case for comfort, she rocked back and forth on the floor. The familiar wood under her cheek felt like her mother's embrace. She waited; certain her mother would sweep into the room and say it had all been a mistake. But she never came.

Suddenly, crashing and clattering erupted from downstairs. Still hugging her violin, Camilla rushed to the staircase.

The scene below seared itself into her young heart: her father raging, tearing photographs from the walls, smashing glass, hurling mementos into the fireplace. Music sheets, jewelry, baubles—all consumed by flame. At the bottom of the pile, her mother's peasant skirt melted bead by bead, its colors blackening in the fire.

"No! Why are you burning Mommy?" Camilla screamed.

Charles shoved her aside roughly. "Go to bed. This is not your concern."

Her eyes, wild with terror, locked on the one thing left in her arms—her violin. Charles' gaze followed hers. In a frenzy, he grabbed at it.

"NO!" She clung to it with every ounce of strength in her small body. They struggled, father and child, until the wood cracked, the top of the violin splitting and hanging limp.

Charles froze, suddenly aware of what he had done—what she had seen. He released the instrument and turned his back, too ashamed to meet her eyes.

Little Camilla sat weeping on the floor, whispering into the hollow of the broken wood, "No... my Johnnii..." But no one heard her. No one ever heard her again.

The memory faded, leaving her in the present with the scraps of the torn newsletter on her bed. For the first time, Camilla realized she had misunderstood. Her father had never known what the violin truly meant—that it was more than wood and strings, that it was her last tether to her mother. She had never told him. It had been their secret, hers and her mothers alone.

Still, the guilt pressed heavy. "I was wrong to hide it," she murmured. "But worse—I was wrong to let him win."

She tore open her closet doors, pushing aside the rows of navy suits and white blouses that symbolized his world. Tossing clothes to the floor, she searched until her hands closed around a silk hanger wrapped in plastic.

"Yes." Her breath caught.

She ripped the plastic away, revealing a burgundy skirt embroidered with crimson flowers and a rose-colored blouse with puffed sleeves and floral buttons. It was her mother's.

She dressed quickly, the fabric molding to her form as though it had been waiting for this day. Her hair tumbled loose from its pins, wild and free. A stroke of red lipstick and a dash of mascara completed the transformation.

At the door, she hesitated. Then she slipped on soft velvet shoes patterned in bright colors, wrapped herself in a shawl, and darted down the staircase.

No one saw her leave.

# CHAPTER 27

His black limousine pulled up to the curb, and Charles sat in silence, waiting for the driver to open the door. The pristine black interior, the smoky glass windows, the faint scent of leather polish—all of it felt like a cage more than a comfort.

But his thoughts didn't turn to the stack of meetings awaiting him. Instead, they circled back to the sharp words with Camilla that morning. Another fight. Another fracture. For one brief moment, he almost admitted to himself that perhaps he had been too harsh, too controlling. Then a cold shiver traveled up his spine, and the past returned to him with brutal clarity.

The foyer. The argument. The first and only time he had struck his wife.

**FLASHBACK**

"Please, Charley," Viola had pleaded as she followed him down the stairs, her skirt brushing the polished banister. "This is important to me—can't you understand that?"

"No, I can't understand!" His voice was sharp, cruel. "You have a daughter and a husband who need you at home. I need you to be here, to greet my business associates as a proper wife should. I need you to take care of Camilla. I need you to grow up and be a wife, God damn it!"

"How dare you!" Her dark eyes had filled with tears, though her voice did not falter. "You know I have never left Camilla with a nanny, never. I have always been with her."

Charles had ignored the truth in her words. "You are my wife. And I don't like this. I need you home."

"But you knew when you married me I was not a trophy wife," she answered, the steel in her voice rising. "You knew I wanted to dance. This is a small theater, four nights a week. I would be home the rest of the time. Please, Charley, come with me. Support me."

"Support you?" His rage boiled over. "What about supporting me? This house, this life—*I* gave you everything. You *are* a trophy wife, whether you admit it or not. I pulled you out of the gutter and gave you all of this. Don't forget that."

Her face flamed red. "Charley, how could you? I don't care about this house or the money—it's corrupted you. I am not, and never will be, a trophy wife."

Crack.

His hand had flown across her cheek before he even registered the movement. The sound echoed in the vaulted foyer. Viola crumpled to the floor, clutching her swollen face, and when she looked up at him with tear-streaked eyes, her silence was more devastating than any words. She rose without another sound, pulled on her coat, and walked out the door.

He had not stopped her.

He had never forgiven himself.

**PRESENT DAY**

Sitting in the limo now, staring out at the gray city morning, Charles muttered under his breath: *I lost her. I will never let the same thing happen to my daughter. Never.*

"Mr. Huntington?" The driver's voice broke through his thoughts. "May I help you out?"

"No." Charles shoved the hand away. "I am not some old man. Leave me."

He climbed out on his own, squaring his shoulders, straightening his tie. He looked up at the bold letters etched into the façade of the bank tower:

**GLOBAL BANK AND TRUST – YOUR FAMILY BANK IN YOUR TOWN, WE ARE ALWAYS HERE FOR YOU.**

Charles smirked at the irony. *Always here for you.* The words rang hollow. But the day was waiting, the agents were circling, and his role had to be played.

With his mask firmly in place, Charles walked through the gleaming double doors.

# CHAPTER 28

The winding iron stairwell curled upward, every ornate carving cool beneath Camilla's fingertips as she climbed. Her mother's blouse clung softly to her, the burgundy skirt swishing around her ankles, and the scarf Johnny had given her floated from her shoulders like a banner. She felt transformed, as if the weight of her father's world had slipped from her shoulders the moment she left the house.

Johnny opened the door before she knocked.

For a long moment he simply stared. His big brown eyes, swept over her and held. His lips parted slightly, as though he had forgotten how to breathe.

"Camilla…" His voice was barely a whisper. "You look like you stepped out of a painting."

The loft glowed around her, its riot of colors and clutter suddenly alive in a way it had never been before. The flowers on the windowsill seemed brighter, the canvases on the walls more vivid. Even the portrait of Johnny's grandfather above the fireplace seemed to smile more broadly in her presence.

Camilla's cheeks warmed. "You're staring. Do I look strange?"

"Strange?" Johnny shook his head slowly, a smile curving across his lips. "No. You look… incredible."

She laughed nervously, brushing at the folds of her skirt. "It's just something of my mother's. I—needed to wear it today."

Johnny set his sketchbook aside without opening it. "Keep it on," he said quietly. "Don't change a thing. I want to paint you like this."

Camilla felt the weight of his words settle into her chest, soft but profound. She set her violin case down on the antique sea chest and let herself sink into the couch. The scarf slipped down her shoulder, and Johnny, without thinking, reached forward to adjust it. His fingers brushed her skin, warm and fleeting, leaving her shivering.

The loft was quiet, save for the ticking of the old clock and the muted hum of life from the streets below. Camilla closed her eyes, and for just a moment, she heard it again—soft notes rising like smoke from the violin, and her mother's voice:

*Let the music open your heart.*

Johnny finally broke the stillness, grabbing his sketchbook and perching on the edge of the trunk-turned-coffee table. His pencil moved fast, his eyes darting from her to the page, capturing every angle of her skirt, the scarf spilling across her shoulder, the lift of her chin.

"Don't move," he murmured. "This—this is the Camilla I want on canvas."

She tried to sit still, but his gaze made her fidget. "You're staring again," she teased. "It's unnerving."

He smirked without looking up. "Get used to it. An artist is allowed to stare at his subject."

"Well," she said, folding her arms, "what if your subject doesn't like being stared at?"

Johnny looked up then, his big brown eyes glinting with mischief. "Then the subject should stop being so distracting."

Camilla laughed, shaking her head. "You're impossible."

"Maybe," he said, dropping the sketchbook onto the couch and standing suddenly, "but I know how to fix a restless model."

Before she could protest, Johnny crossed the room in two strides and reached for her hands. "Come on."

"What are you doing?"

"Dance with me," he said simply.

"Dance? Here?" She looked around at the cluttered loft.

"Yes, here." He pulled her up from the loveseat, her skirt swirling as she stumbled into his arms. "We'll clear a space." With a gentle sweep, he nudged the beanbag chair aside with his foot and guided her into the middle of the room.

There was no music—until she realized her violin was still open on the trunk. As though answering the moment, a note seemed to hum faintly in her ears, that same old melody, her mother's voice lingering: but surprisingly the whisper words changed *"Let the dance set you free"*.

Johnny didn't seem to notice, but he moved with surprising grace, spinning her gently, one hand at her waist, the other steady at her back. Camilla laughed, the sound bubbling up freely, her earlier tension dissolving.

"You're not so bad at this," she admitted breathlessly.

"I told you," Johnny grinned, leaning in close, "I have many talents."

They spun once more, then collapsed onto the couch, tangled in laughter. His hand brushed a strand of hair from her cheek, his touch lingering. For a heartbeat, the world fell silent.

Then his lips found hers—soft at first, almost questioning, then warmer, playful, insistent. She kissed him back, laughing against his mouth as he whispered between kisses, "See? Much better than sitting still."

Their laughter faded, replaced by the soft hum of the city drifting through the windows. Johnny shifted, settling back into the couch, and Camilla found herself tucked against his chest, the steady beat of his heart grounding her in a way nothing else had in years.

The scarf slipped from her shoulder, pooling across both like a shared secret. His arm circled her waist, his thumb tracing idle patterns against the fabric of her skirt. Neither spoke. They didn't need to.

Camilla's eyes grew heavy, lulled by the warmth of his embrace and the faint ghost of a melody that drifted at the edges of her awareness. Somewhere beyond the loft, beyond even Johnny, she heard her mother's voice, tender and insistent:

*Let the music open your heart. Let the dance set you free*

She smiled softly, surrendering to the sound. Johnny pressed a kiss against her hairline, lingering as though reluctant to let go, then closed his own eyes.

As the sun slipped below the rooftops and the room turned golden with dusk, they drifted into sleep—two worlds colliding quietly, wrapped in each other's arms.

# CHAPTER 29

Charles rode quietly in the back of the limo, watching the familiar streets roll by. His gaze snagged, as always, on the old cemetery. The iron gates loomed, the gravestones stark against the morning fog. Every instinct told him to turn away, but he forced himself to look.

"Do you always have to go this route and pass that damn place with all the nameless, faceless dead?" he barked suddenly at the driver.

"Sorry, sir. Going around takes an extra thirty minutes," the driver replied, his tone flat from years of the same question.

Charles grunted, not answering. He shifted in his seat, staring at the watch on his wrist, calculating the hours until his next appointment, until the next disaster.

For two weeks, the FBI had paraded through his bank like vultures. The gray-suited men with their expressionless eyes tore through records, upended compliance files, and unnerved his employees. Staff had begun to call in sick, some never returning. And then—just as suddenly as they had arrived—they were gone, leaving behind only scraps of paper, coffee cups, and the lingering dread of men who could return at any time.

Now the bank felt hollow. The marble lobby echoed with too few voices, clocks ticking above an uneasy silence. It was in that silence that Charles ran into Michael.

The staff clung together in nervous clumps, their loyalty fragile. Charles stood before them with his brightest smile and smoothest tone.

"Thank you, everyone, for your dedication during these last two weeks. The interruption was unnecessary, and I assure you there will be no serious repercussions. A few accounts slipped through compliance. That's all. We are handling it."

Michael stepped forward, smiling broadly, his voice warm. "And to thank you for your loyalty, there will be a special bonus in your paychecks this week."

The staff turned toward him, relief lighting their faces. They shook his hand, thanked him, clung to him as the reassuring hero while Charles simmered.

As soon as they were gone, Charles leaned in, his voice low and dangerous. "Meet me in my office. Now."

The elevator carried them directly into his vast corner office. Charles didn't wait for pleasantries—he moved straight to the liquor cabinet, poured two tumblers of Scotch, and drained his in a single gulp. His shoulders sagged, then lifted as he snapped his gaze to Michael.

"You son of a bitch. You told me you'd get them past compliance."

Michael leaned back, swirling his drink lazily. "Now, now, Charles. You can't blame this on me. I did my part. I even managed to turn the staff around today. You saw that."

Charles slammed his empty glass down. "I just hope this is over."

"Of course it is," Michael replied smoothly. "At worst? A fine, a slap on the wrist. Remember, we're the small arm of a very large and very powerful international bank."

But Charles wasn't listening. His thoughts drifted. Camilla. Always Camilla. The Gypsy magazine torn in pieces. The silence between them since. Her careful evasions, her constant absences.

Michael noticed his distraction. "Is this about your daughter again?"

Charles clenched his jaw. "It's nothing."

"Oh, it's something. She's been seen across town at that little music shop. Not just once. Today." Michael's grin widened. "And she's not there for the old man, either. There's someone else—a boy. Lives upstairs."

Charles shot forward, grabbing Michael by the throat, rage flooding his veins. "What are you talking about?"

Michael wheezed, laughing through the choke. "Relax. She's seeing someone. Don't shoot the messenger."

Charles's fist connected with his jaw before he could finish. Blood smeared Michael's lip, but his grin remained. "Feel better now, pops? I can take care of it if you want. Just say the word."

Charles staggered back, memories flooding him—Viola's dark eyes pleading in the foyer, his own hand flying across her face, her coat disappearing out the door. He had promised himself it would never happen again. Not to Camilla.

"No," he rasped. "I'll deal with her myself. No trouble. Not from you."

Michael smirked, straightening his tie with bloody fingers. "Fine. Just remember—you need me right now."

Charles turned away, sinking into his leather chair. Michael's words—*the small arm of a very large bank*—echoed, and with them came the memory of another office, another confrontation, fifteen years earlier...

# CHAPTER 30

**Fifteen Years Ago**

The gleaming skyscraper dominated the city skyline, its glass façade reflecting the sharp morning sun. Fifteen years earlier, a young Charles Huntington strode through its marble lobby, his tailored suit pressed, his polished briefcase clutched like a shield. He had rehearsed this meeting in his mind a dozen times, but nothing steadied the nervous tremor in his chest.

After a swift elevator ride to the executive floor, Charles approached the dark mahogany desk where Natalie, Raptnor's assistant, sat poised, her fingers hovering over the receiver like a sentinel.

"Good morning, Mr. Huntington," she said, her professional smile as practiced as his. "How may I help you?"

"Is Emmet available? I need to speak with him urgently."

"Let me check." Natalie lifted the receiver, her voice crisp. "Mr. Raptnor? Mr. Huntington is here to see you." A pause, then a nod. "Yes, sir. At once. Shall I bring coffee?" She rose and gestured toward the imposing double doors. "Mr. Raptnor will see you now."

Charles hesitated at the threshold, shoulders momentarily slumped. But with each step deeper into the office, he straightened his spine and forced brightness into his expression.

"Good day, Emmet. Beautiful morning, isn't it?"

Raptnor leaned back in his leather chair, his eyes sharp. "You're unusually cheerful. I take it the mall development is proceeding as planned?"

Charles's smile faltered. "That's actually why I'm here. We've hit a… small complication."

"Complication?" Raptnor's voice hardened.

"One homeowner refuses to sell. I offered well above market value, but he insists it's his family home. Generations of memories—"

Raptnor rose abruptly, silencing him with a raised hand. "Then we pursue alternative measures."

"Alternative measures, sir?" Charles's collar tightened.

"Legal maneuvers. Eminent domain. A few signatures and your problem disappears." Raptnor's tone was casual, like he was discussing the weather.

"But we're talking about someone's life, their heritage—"

"Charles." Raptnor circled the desk and placed a heavy hand on his shoulder. "I've mentored you, elevated you through this organization. Haven't I?"

Charles nodded reluctantly.

"Then remember this above all else: you serve the bank and its clients. Sentiment is a luxury you cannot afford. Principles don't pay for penthouses."

"But sir, you don't understand…" Charles faltered.

Raptnor cut him off with a dismissive wave. "What I understand is this: your family prospers when you follow my directives. Your wife, your new baby—they deserve comfort, luxury. Isn't that what you want for them?"

Charles saw Viola's face in his mind, their infant daughter nestled in her arms, sunlight streaming through the nursery window. The choice crystallized before him.

"You're right, sir," he said finally, his voice hollow. "Consider it done."

As he left the office, he felt invisible threads tightening around him. A gilded cage, willingly entered.

## PRESENT DAY

The memory dissolved. Charles sat at his vast walnut desk, the skyline stretching gray and heavy outside his office window. Fifteen years had passed, but Raptnor's words still echoed like iron shackles: *Principles don't pay for penthouses.*

Now, with FBI investigations circling, staff whispering, and his daughter slipping through his fingers, he felt the walls of that gilded cage closing in. His fingers tightened around the receiver.

"After all these years, Emmett, you owe me this one," he whispered.

"Sylvia," he barked, "get Emmet Raptnor on the phone immediately. Tell him it's urgent."

"Yes, sir." Sylvia's hands trembled slightly as she punched in the familiar number. A crisp click answered.

"Mr. Raptnor's office," came Natalie's efficient voice, unchanged by the years.

Sylvia chimed in, "Natalie, I have Charles Huntington for Mr. Raptnor." She handed the receiver over.

Charles cleared his throat, forcing steadiness into his tone. "Natalie, it's Charles Huntington. I need to speak with Emmett immediately. It's a matter of some urgency."

There was a pause—measured, deliberate. The faint scratch of a pen on paper, the shuffle of distant footsteps.

"Please hold, Mr. Huntington."

The line went silent, nothing but the faint hiss of static filling the void. Charles sat rigid in his chair, the weight of fifteen years pressing against his chest. Every second stretched taut, a string ready to snap.

Then—

*Click.*

# CHAPTER 31

Michael's rise through the bank's hierarchy had always raised eyebrows. He was too smooth, too quick

 make problems vanish. But no one dared question him—not when quarterly profits soared under his watch. Problems disappeared; numbers rose. That was all the board needed to know.

Tonight, under the sickly glow of a flickering streetlamp, Michael looked like a different man altogether. The polished veneer of the banker had been stripped away. The silk of his tailored suit seemed harder, his jaw tighter, his eyes colder. This was the Michael no boardroom would ever see.

"Jimmy," he called into the alley.

From the shadows, a hulking figure stepped forward, hands shoved into his overcoat pockets. "Been a slow week. Got something for me?"

Michael's voice dropped to a businesslike monotone. "A small job. Right up your alley. Easy money."

Jimmy laughed. "Easy money's my favorite kind. What's the catch?"

"No catch. I want you to deliver a message. There's a kid—Johnny Oshay. Lives in a loft above the old repair shop on Fifth Street. You give him this check, tell him to cash it, and disappear. No questions asked."

Jimmy's lips twisted. "Disappear from where?"

"Not a where—a who. A girl. He knows which one."

Jimmy rocked back on his heels. "That's it? Payoff job? Sounds too clean."

"If he doesn't take the offer," Michael added, eyes narrowing, "convince him. Don't hurt him if you can help it—but if you need to get a little rough, so be it. Just... resolve the problem."

Jimmy nodded, his grin sharp and feral. "Consider it done, boss."

# CHAPTER 32

Johnny grabbed his coat and hopped down the winding stairs two at a time, quickly arriving at the bottom.

"Hey, what is the hurry, John?" Mr. Hempshaw called after him.

Johnny smiled back at him and replied, "I have a lot to do and must be home early. I, uh, have company tonight." His smile widened, thinking of Camilla.

Mr. Hempshaw just smirked and smiled. "I see!"

Johnny ran down the street to the coffee shop on the corner. He walked in and went up to the display case of aromatic coffees, from light to dark. Without hesitation, knowing just the bag he wanted, Johnny reached over to pick up the dark espresso European blend and took it to the counter.

"Good day to you, Maria," he said to the young Latina girl at the counter. "How are you this fine fall day? I see you got out your winter sweater—very pretty in green, Maria!"

She just giggled with a schoolgirl crush smile. "Thank you, Johnny! That will be $5.25 please." As he handed her $6.00, saying, "And keep the change darlin'," she just melted.

Johnny ran out the door, leaving Maria swooning behind him. He walked slower now, knowing he had time before Camilla's arrival.

Cutting through the alleyway, the shortcut he always used to take back to the shop, he felt a presence behind him. Someone was walking behind him, and as he sped up, so did this person.

He was never concerned or afraid in this neighborhood, as he knew everyone that lived around here. Despite the shabby look of some of the building exteriors, they were filled with artisans, musicians, and painters, and not a bit of violence ran through their bones.

So with that thought, he stopped and turned around to look right into his pursuer's face. Jimmy was a big rough character, wearing an overcoat and holding both hands in his pockets as if to hide something.

Johnny had always been brave and bold, and although he felt a slight flutter in his stomach, he decided not to waste time and find out what this guy wanted.

"Uh, hello... You don't look like you are from this neighborhood."

"No, buddy, I am not, but maybe you can help me? I am looking for John Oshay. Do you know him?" he said as he walked up close to Johnny, looking directly at him without flinching.

"Well, you are in luck. I am John Oshay," Johnny said, his voice a bit shaky. "If you plan to rob me, I wouldn't waste your time. I have very little cash and a bag of coffee beans worth about five bucks. Um, would really not be worth the hassle." He nervously laughed.

"Hey!" Jimmy said, getting a bit angry. "I'm no petty thief. I am here to make you a deal—maybe a deal you can't refuse," he concluded, putting on his worst Godfather imitation.

"What kind of deal?" asked Johnny.

"I hear tell that you have a little uptown sweetie you been romancing up in that artsy-fartsy loft you live in. Well, there are a couple of very influential men who don't like it. You had your fun with her; now it's time to move on back downtown, if you know what I mean?" He wiggled his finger in his coat pocket to look like a gun barrel.

"Excuse me, Mr.—what is your name?"

"You can call me Mr. X."

"Oh, ok, Mr. X—that is quite 1950s clever." Johnny laughed. "I don't think it is up to the influential uptown men to tell me who I can see or not see. I don't work for them."

"Yeah, but I do." As he reached into his pocket and started pulling something out, Johnny thought maybe he had overstepped his bounds, but to his surprise, Mr. X pulled out a piece of paper—a check.

"Here is the deal, kid. You take this check, cash it, and go away. Lock your door next time she comes by or just be a brave little guy and tell her you moved on. Got it?"

"No, I don't got it, and I don't like your deal. You think I can be bought off like the uptown employees? Well, think again."

"Now who's being a 1950s cliché," said Jimmy, shoving the check at Johnny. "Don't be stupid, kid. At least look at the check before you turn it down."

Johnny snatched the paper, more to see than to accept. His eyes landed on the number—and for a brief second, his breath caught. It was obscene, the kind of sum bankers and politicians ruined lives for.

But not him. Not Johnny. Money meant nothing in this moment.

His stomach turned—not with temptation, but with rage. The check wasn't an offer. It was a threat.

"They know about Camilla," he thought. "If this is their opening move, what comes next?"

He folded the check slowly, forcing himself not to rip it in two.

"I don't work for uptown men. And I sure as hell don't sell out the people I care about," Johnny said, his voice tight.

"Suit yourself," Mr. X replied, already turning away. Over his shoulder, he added, "Think it over, kid. The next deal won't be so sweet."

Johnny stood frozen in the alley, the check burning in his hand. For the first time in years, he felt the weight of real danger—not for himself, but for her.

# CHAPTER 33

Johnny entered his loft, coat sliding from his shoulders as he tossed the coffee beans onto the counter. He sat on the couch and unfolded the check once more. The numbers stared back at him, obscene in their size.

But it wasn't the money.

It was the message. Someone knew about Camilla. Someone with reach, with power, and with no hesitation about buying—or breaking—whatever stood in their way.

Johnny pressed the check flat against his knee, his jaw tightening. *"If I tell her, she'll panic. She'll never come back. She deserves beauty, freedom, not shadows following her every step. This isn't her burden—it's mine."*

He tossed the check casually on the counter. Out of sight, but not out of mind.

Yawning, he realized how tired he was; it had been a long day. He laid his head against the large fluffy pillow on the couch and slowly closed his eyes, drifting off to sleep.

A loud knock on the door suddenly woke him up. He jumped up quickly, remembering about his expected company, and opened the door to see Camilla standing there. She looked unlike she ever had before—dressed unusually romantic for the season, in a flowing wool skirt, a fitted coat cinched at the waist, and tall leather boots. A wide-brimmed felt hat, soft gray with a ribbon band, sat atop her long dark hair, which spilled in waves over her shoulders. The outfit had a timeless elegance, almost dreamlike.

She tugged the hat off with one swift motion, tossed it across the room, and then leaped into his arms, pressing her lips to his in a kiss so full of longing that it stole his breath.

"Hello, Johnny," she said in a sultry voice, her green eyes shining.

Johnny was stunned, then glanced over to see the check sitting on the table, growing larger and larger like in a cartoon.

"Uh, Camilla, I need to tell you something," he began, looking into her beautiful eyes, which appeared sad. The room started closing in on him, the check getting larger and larger, and he just looked in her eyes as she faded away...

"No, no!" Johnny's screams woke him up, and he sat up straight on the couch—

*KNOCK-KNOCK.*

Holding his head in his hands, he muttered, "Oh no, I didn't know I was that tired, shit!" He looked at the clock, which said 1 p.m.

"Just a minute, I will be right there," he called to the door. He quickly grabbed the check and shoved it deep into the kitchen drawer, opened the bag of coffee beans to let the aroma fill the room, and ran his fingers through his disheveled hair.

When he opened the door, Camilla stood there in a big gray wool sweater, her cheeks flushed pink from the cold, and a bright scarf wound around her head and neck. But Johnny froze for a second—he saw she was holding a hat, dangling down her right side, a brimmed gray felt hat, the very image of the one from his dream.

"Hi," she said with a shy smile. "It is very chilly out there. Hey, did I wake you? You look like you just got up."

"Yeah," Johnny admitted with a smile, still shaken but trying not to show it. "I'm not great at cat naps. But I'm glad you're here."

She stepped in, looking around the loft as if it were a second home now. Johnny moved behind her, tugged her scarf gently into place, and brushed a kiss against her lips.

"No painting today," he whispered. "There's somewhere else I want to take you."

She looked up at him, puzzled but trusting. "Where?"

"You'll see," he said, grabbing his coat. "But I promise—you'll love it."

He didn't tell her about the check. Not yet.

# CHAPTER 34

Johnny tugged his coat tighter and adjusted the scarf around Camilla's neck, then settled the hat over her hair, straightening the brim before guiding her gently toward the stairwell. The ironwork spiraled downward, ornate carvings casting lace-like shadows along the walls under the dim bulbs above. Their footsteps echoed as they descended, until they spilled out onto the street where the cool air brushed Camilla's cheeks.

"Where are we going?" she asked, her voice a mix of curiosity and nerves.

"You'll see," Johnny said, a mischievous glint in his eyes.

They walked arm in arm, boots clicking against the uneven pavement, past shuttered shops and faded murals. The city seemed quieter here, as if holding its breath. When they turned down an alley that looked unremarkable—just weathered bricks and mud-slick stones—Johnny stopped.

"Most people pass this place without ever seeing it," he whispered. "But if you look the right way, you'll notice it."

Camilla frowned. "Notice what?"

He shifted aside, revealing a faint sliver of light glowing between the bricks. At first, she thought it a trick of the streetlamps. But as she stared, the outline sharpened—an entryway hidden in plain sight. Her breath caught.

Johnny slipped his hand into hers and pulled her through.

On the other side, the world shifted. Cobblestone streets stretched out, lined with shopfronts painted in jewel tones, bright flags fluttering overhead, the air thick with the mingled scents of espresso, bread, and incense. Music floated in fragments—laughter, guitar strings, a violin somewhere in the distance.

Camilla froze, her eyes wide, every nerve alive. "Oh my God," she whispered. "What is this place?"

Johnny's smile softened, as if he had been waiting for this moment. "We call it the Gypsy Lair. It's where we come to live free, to create, to be. No rules, no masks. Just who we are."

Her heart skipped. For the first time in her life, she felt an uncanny pull of belonging—like stepping into a memory she hadn't lived yet but had always carried inside her.

The moment they crossed the threshold, Camilla felt her breath catch. It was as if someone had pulled aside a curtain on reality, revealing a hidden world pulsing with life.

Cobblestones glistened under lantern light, their worn surfaces reflecting hints of color from the banners strung overhead. Bright fabrics rippled in the crisp wind—scarlet, emerald, gold—casting moving shadows across the brick facades. The air smelled of roasted chestnuts, beeswax candles, spiced wine, and incense; the scents wove together into something heady, intoxicating.

Street musicians clustered on corners, violins and guitars battling joyfully with tambourines and drums. Their rhythms collided and then harmonized, creating unpredictable music that tugged at the heart more than the ears. A girl with copper braids spun in a circle, her skirts a whirl of peacock blue, while a pair of raucous boys wearing blue jeans and denim jackets ran past, their laughter echoing like bells.

Camilla tilted her head back to see strings of glass lanterns strung like constellations above the narrow street. Each lantern glowed in a different hue—amber, sapphire, rose—casting pools of color on faces as strangers smiled at each other without hesitation, without suspicion.

She clutched Johnny's arm tighter. "It feels... alive," she whispered, her eyes darting from a painter splashing crimson across a half-finished canvas to a dancer who leapt into the street with ribbons tied to her wrists, ribbons that painted the air itself.

Johnny leaned closer. "This is what life looks like when no one is pretending."

Her heart squeezed. For the first time, she could feel the difference—not just see it. Her father's house was a museum of appearances, marble and glass polished to a cold shine. But here, even the broken cobbles seemed to breathe.

Camilla slowed, almost afraid to blink in case it all disappeared. A guitarist struck a bold chord and someone began singing in a language she didn't understand, yet the melody wrapped around her like an embrace. She thought she heard her mother's voice threading through the song: *Let the dance set you free.*

# CHAPTER 35

Johnny guided Camilla through the winding street until they stopped before a low doorway tucked beneath a cascade of ivy. A carved wooden sign swung gently in the breeze:

**Caffè di Giovanni**

The windows glowed amber, fogged at the edges from the warmth within.

The moment they stepped inside, a wall of scents wrapped around her—freshly ground espresso beans, orange zest, almond biscotti, melted chocolate. The café was alive with voices: an old man arguing passionately about art movements, a group of girls singing softly at a corner table, a violin bow scraping a half-tuned scale in the back.

Johnny slipped his arm from hers only to wave broadly at the owner, a silver-haired gentleman with dark, kind eyes and a mustache curled like a ribbon. "Giovanni!" Johnny's voice boomed with affection. "I've brought someone special to meet you, her name is Camilla"

Giovanni wiped his hands on a linen cloth and came forward, bowing gallantly as if she were royalty. "Signorina Camilla," he said warmly, his accent rolling like music, "anyone Johnny calls special is family to me. Welcome, welcome."

Camilla blushed under his gaze. "Thank you. I've heard your espresso is legendary."

　　　　　　　　　　　　　　

Giovanni's eyes twinkled. "Ah, Johnny has already ruined the surprise. But no matter—you will taste and know for yourself. Sit, both of you."

He ushered them to a tiny table tucked in a corner beneath a shelf stacked with painted ceramic cups and jars of honey. Candles flickered in colored glass holders, staining their faces with ruby and sapphire light.

As Giovanni bustled to prepare the espresso, Camilla looked around, enchanted. Every table was crowded with artists and dreamers: a poet scribbling in a notebook, a seamstress mending a bright skirt, two lovers whispering close enough their foreheads touched. There was no pretense here, no rigid rules. Just living.

Johnny leaned across the table, his big brown eyes catching hers in the glow. "See? This is the world I wanted you to know."

Giovanni returned moments later, bearing a tray. Two small cups of espresso, pitchers of thick cream warmed to silk, a bowl of sugar cubes, and—balanced precariously on the edge of the tray—a plate of almond biscotti dusted with powdered sugar.

"Half espresso, half cream," Giovanni instructed as he poured. "No sugar unless your heart insists. The cream, she is sweet enough." He winked at Camilla, who laughed and felt the heat rise in her cheeks.

The first sip was like velvet—dark, bitter, and then soothed into richness by the cream. Camilla closed her eyes, savoring. "Oh, my..."

Johnny grinned. "Told you."

Giovanni beamed, hands on his hips. "Ah, bella, now you are truly one of us."

Giovanni lingered at their table, watching with satisfaction as Camilla sipped her espresso and smiled. He tapped his finger on the tray as though keeping time to an invisible rhythm. Then, with sudden resolve, he snapped his fingers.

"Wait here," he said, eyes sparkling. "I have something—*something molto speciale.*"

Before Camilla could ask, he bustled away toward the far wall, where a tall brocade cabinet stood like a shrine. He pulled open its carved wooden doors to reveal a collection of instruments—violins, violas, cellos, each glistening with polish and age, their scrolls and curves catching the candlelight like amber jewels.

Camilla gasped softly. "Oh, Johnny..."

Johnny leaned closer, murmuring in her ear, "I told you this place has magic hidden in every corner."

Giovanni's hands hovered reverently before selecting one particular violin. Its body was a rich sienna, its edges worn smooth by decades of playing. The carved scroll was delicate, almost floral in design, as though the maker had poured his soul into its creation. Giovanni cradled it as though carrying a child, and when he turned, his eyes were gleaming.

"Signorina," he said, his accent caressing every syllable, "a musician must never drink coffee without offering something in return. Play for us. Let us hear the music in your heart."

Camilla froze, staring at Johnny with a whisper "what did you do?"

Johnny just smiled, shrugged his shoulders and played dumb.

Camilla looked back at the extraordinary instrument "Oh—I couldn't possibly. I—I don't even have my own violin with me."

"This one will serve," Giovanni said, lowering it into her arms. His voice softened, coaxing. "Feel her weight. She remembers every hand that has held her. She will remember yours, too."

The wood was warm against her skin, startlingly alive, as if it had been waiting for her. Her breath caught. Johnny was already at her side, steadying the bow in her trembling fingers.

"You can do this," he whispered, his lips so close she felt the brush of his breath against her ear. "Just close your eyes. Let it happen."

Camilla obeyed. The violin nestled into the curve of her shoulder like it belonged there. She drew the bow across the strings, hesitant at first. A thin, trembling note quivered in the air. She faltered—then, faintly, she felt another presence. A familiar warmth enveloped her, a hand that wasn't Johnny's guiding her.

Her mother.

"*Let the dance set you free,*" came the whispered echo, as soft and sure as breath against her cheek.

The note steadied, deepened. Her fingers found the strings as though guided by memory older than her own. A melody unfurled, winding and rich, spilling into the café. It grew bolder with each stroke, weaving gypsy rhythms into the chatter of voices, pulling the room into its current.

Johnny's hand lingered lightly at her back, anchoring her. Her body began to sway with the rhythm, her bow hand moving faster, her soul carried into the music. The café fell silent, every conversation hushed, every cup poised midair as all eyes fixed on her.

Then her body lifted with the music—she rose to her feet, the violin singing wild and free, her skirt swishing as she turned with the rhythm. She became movement itself: twirling, stepping, bow flying like a ribbon in her hand. The melody swelled and crashed like waves, lifting her higher than she thought possible.

When the final note broke into silence, Camilla stood breathless, her chest heaving, the violin trembling in her grip.

A heartbeat later, applause erupted, thunderous and joyous. Giovanni clapped the loudest, his laughter booming. "*Bellissima!*" he declared, wiping tears from his eyes. "You have given us a gift tonight. *La musica di tua anima.* The music of your soul."

Camilla blushed, overwhelmed, and glanced at Johnny. He was looking at her as though she were the only person in the world, his eyes alight with pride and something deeper—recognition.

The applause still lingered in the air as Giovanni bustled back behind the counter, humming one of the melodies she had played. A few moments later, he returned, balancing a tray as though it carried a holy relic.

"Here, for our star tonight," he said, carefully setting down two steaming cups of fresh espresso. Alongside them rested a small porcelain dish piled with golden biscotti, their edges glistening with sugar and almonds. Two tiny pitchers of thick cream accompanied the cups, their surfaces swirling with ribbons of steam.

"*Per voi.* For you. No charge, of course. The music you gave us tonight is more precious than money." His eyes softened as he added, "Your mother would be proud."

Camilla's hand froze halfway to the saucer. She looked at him quickly, startled. "My mother?"

Giovanni only smiled, tapping his temple knowingly before walking away, leaving her with the words hanging between them like incense.

Johnny reached for the pitcher of cream. "Here, let me." He poured a silken stream into her cup, the white cloud blooming and curling through the dark espresso like smoke unfurling in water. "See? Even coffee dances here."

Camilla smiled faintly, watching the pattern dissolve. Her fingers trembled as she took the cup, but Johnny steadied her hand, his warm touch grounding her. She sipped, and the flavor was unlike anything she had ever tasted—deep, rich, softened by the heavy cream, each note of flavor resonant like a chord struck on her violin.

"Mmm," she sighed. "This might be better than your espresso after all."

Johnny clutched his chest in mock agony. "You wound me, *bella*. I'll never recover."

She laughed, breaking the heaviness, and reached for one of the biscotti. It crunched sweetly between her teeth, almonds and sugar mingling with the bitter-smooth coffee. She leaned back, letting herself sink into the cozy corner, the hum of voices and faint strains of music wrapping her like a shawl.

Johnny studied her in silence, his eyes soft, proud, almost reverent. Finally, he leaned closer, his lips brushing her ear. "See? This is your world, Camilla. You fit here, like music fits in silence."

Her heart fluttered. For once, she didn't resist the thought. She only smiled and let herself believe it might be true.

After finishing the last crumbs of biscotti, Camilla dabbed her lips with the linen napkin and leaned back, glowing from within. Johnny caught the spark in her eyes and grinned.

"Come on," he said, offering his hand. "There's one more place I want you to see before the night takes over."

# CHAPTER 36

They slipped back into the narrow street, weaving through the clusters of musicians and artisans. Lanterns glowed overhead, their colored glass spilling patches of blue, red, and gold onto the cobblestones. Then Johnny stopped before a weathered wooden sign, hand-painted in curling letters:

**Lazlo's Gypsy Bazaar**

"Oh!" Camilla exclaimed, her eyes wide. "We must go in."

Inside, the air was thick with the scent of simmering potatoes, cabbage, and smoked bacon. Shelves climbed to the ceiling, stacked with books, silks, and odd trinkets. Cabinets overflowed with jewelry, fabrics, and carved wooden charms, while garlands of dried flowers dangled from the rafters.

A small man with sharp eyes sat behind a desk made from rough-hewn firewood. "Welcome, welcome. You must be new," Lazlo said in a rich, accented voice.

"Yes, thank you," Camilla replied politely, her eyes darting over the treasures. "May I ask... what is that smell? It's delightful."

The man chuckled. "Only a Romani would say potato and cabbage smell delightful. Are you Romani, young lady?"

Camilla hesitated, uncertainly. "I don't know. I only know it feels... familiar."

Lazlo studied her for a moment longer but said nothing more, simply ladling a bit of the soup into a carved wooden cup. "Taste. It will warm your bones."

She sipped. The flavor filled her chest with warmth, so startlingly familiar it nearly brought tears to her eyes. "Johnny, taste this!" she urged, passing him the cup.

As he did, her gaze wandered to the shelves of books. Something tugged at her. "By chance... do you have anything on an old violinist? Janos Borza?" she asked.

At once Lazlo's eyes lit with recognition. "Ahh... Janos Borza." He climbed a tall ladder, coughing as he retrieved a dust-laden leather volume. Wiping the cover, he revealed golden embossed letters: **The Forgotten Music of Janos Borza**.

Camilla opened it carefully, turning pages until she froze, her breath catching. There, in a sepia photograph, was the violin—her Johnnii— gleaming and new. "Johnny... look! That's it. That's my violin."

Johnny leaned close, his arm brushing hers. "Well, I'll be damned," he murmured. "What are the odds?"

Her eyes brimmed with awe. "Mr. Lazlo, I must buy this book. How much?"

"For you... fifty dollars."

Before Johnny could reach for his wallet, Camilla pressed her own money into Lazlo's palm. "This is my treasure. Thank you."

Lazlo wrapped the book with care. As they turned to leave, he said softly, "That violin carries stories, young lady. Don't ignore them."

The door creaked open, and as they stepped outside, a sound like rolling thunder met their ears. Music. Tambourines, violins, clarinets—wild and jubilant. The narrow street was suddenly a river of color.

A dozen women in jewel-toned skirts spun at the procession's head, their laughter ringing above the beat of hand drums. Men followed with brass instruments, some swaying drunkenly, others solemn, while children darted between them, tossing handfuls of flower petals. At the center, an ornate carriage, draped in crimson cloth, carried a coffin gilded with gold.

"What is this?" Camilla whispered, clutching Johnny's arm.

"A Romani funeral," Lazlo's voice drifted from the shop doorway behind them. "In our tradition, death is not darkness—it is a dance. We send the spirit on with color and music. Each mourner will whisper forgiveness at the grave. Only then can the departed rest."

Camilla's heart raced. The swirl of colors, the pulse of the music, the raw joy braided with sorrow—it all tugged at something deep in her. A whisper reached her ear, soft and unmistakable:

*"Let the dance set you free."*

Her mother's voice.

She tilted her face up, stars just beginning to appear above the lanterns, and felt Johnny's steady hand at her back. He leaned close and whispered, "Beautiful, isn't it? Death turned into celebration. Like life itself—wild and fleeting, but worth the dance."

Camilla closed her eyes, letting the music carry her. For the first time, she felt she wasn't just visiting Johnny's world—she was living it; she belonged here.

# CHAPTER 37

As Camilla browsed the crowded shop, her fingers trailed across silken scarves folded in neat piles. Rich burgundy, violet, and gold threads shimmered under the lantern light, each one alive with intricate embroidery and tiny mirrored sequins that caught the glow like stars. One scarf stopped her—it was multicolored, patterned in swirls of crimson, turquoise, and amber. For a moment, her breath caught.

Her mother's face flashed before her, laughing in the sunlight, her hair wrapped in a scarf not unlike this one, its ends fluttering as she twirled in dance.

Camilla touched the fabric softly, reverently. "So much like hers..." she whispered to herself, though Johnny caught the words.

"You like that one?" Johnny asked gently, watching the way her fingers lingered.

She quickly pulled her hand away, embarrassed by the sudden surge of emotion. "Oh—it just reminded me of something. Of her. It's silly."

Johnny didn't press. His eyes softened, but he let the moment breathe, simply tucking it away. Lazlo, watching quietly from behind the counter, gave the faintest nod, as if he, too, understood more than he would say.

## *CHAPTER 38*

The music of the procession still lingered in their ears as the last dancers spun out of sight, leaving behind only the shimmer of colored skirts and the faint clatter of drums fading into the distance. Camilla stood in the doorway of Lazlo's shop, clutching her wrapped book, her heart pounding with the sense that she had just glimpsed her true reflection for the first time.

Johnny touched her elbow gently. "Come. The night isn't over yet."

They walked arm in arm beneath lantern-lit arches and over narrow bridges where the water below reflected ripples of flame and starlight. The air smelled of wood smoke, mulled wine, and the faint perfume of winter flowers. Above them, the moon had risen, a burnished gold disc hanging low over the rooftops.

"Look," Johnny whispered, pointing upward as a streak of light split the sky. "A falling star. Quick, make a wish."

She closed her eyes, the chilly air tingling her cheeks. *I wish this feeling could last forever,* she thought. *That I could always feel so alive.*

When she opened her eyes, Johnny was smiling knowingly, as though he had heard her unspoken prayer. "Good," he said softly. "Now let's make it come true."

He led her through an ivy-covered archway, and suddenly the street gave way to a hidden garden bathed in silvery light. Strings of tiny twinkle lights laced through bare branches, and lanterns hung low over a single table set with pewter goblets, linen napkins, and a basket of flowers. Two slender candles flickered at the center, their flames swaying in the night breeze. The air was warmer here, softened by a hidden heater that cast a faint golden glow.

Camilla stopped in her tracks, her lips parted. "Johnny... what is this?"

"This," he said, pulling out her chair with a flourish, "is your wish."

She let him guide her into the seat, still holding her book like a talisman. A bottle of chilled wine waited in a pewter bucket; its surface beaded with condensation. Platters of fruit, cheese, and bread laid out as though awaiting royalty.

Camilla blinked, overwhelmed by the beauty of it, by the sheer thoughtfulness. "Johnny... I don't know what to say."

"You don't have to say anything." He poured the wine, the ruby liquid catching the moonlight. "Just be here. Be alive."

For a while, they talked in soft tones, laughter rising and falling with the flicker of the candles. And then, as though drawn by some unspoken cue, Johnny stood and extended his hand.

"Dance with me."

There was no music at first—just the rustle of leaves, the soft crackle of candles. Then, faintly, from somewhere in the distance, came a melody: a violin threading through the night air. Camilla's breath caught. Her mother's voice whispered again, *"Let the dance set you free."*

Johnny's arms wrapped around her, his warmth enveloping her as they swayed together beneath the stars. Her boots shifted gently over the cobblestones, and she leaned into him, her cheek brushing against his chest. The world melted into rhythm and breath.

When he finally kissed her, it was tender and inevitable, like the final note of a song that had been waiting years to resolve. She kissed him back with equal certainty.

And as the stars wheeled overhead, Camilla knew with a clarity that pierced her heart: this was not an escape, not a rebellion. This was her beginning.

The melody drifted toward them, carried faintly on the night air. Camilla felt her mother's voice stir within her, soft and familiar: *"Let the dance set you free."*

Her breath caught, and instinctively, she leaned over the edge of the bridge, gazing into the dark water below. The surface shimmered as though stirred by invisible hands. For one fleeting moment, she saw her mother's face reflected there, luminous, serene, her eyes full of love. Tiny sparks of light—like stars shaken loose from the sky—rose out of the rippling water, swirling upward before dissolving into the night.

Camilla pressed a hand to her chest, her throat tight with wonder and grief all tangled together. "Mama..." she whispered.

Johnny's arms circled her waist, steadying her as she swayed from the weight of the vision. "I've got you," he murmured against her hair. She leaned back into him, still watching as the last sparkles faded and the water grew still again.

When she turned her face upward to him, her eyes shone with unshed tears, and the world tilted into a rhythm that belonged only to them. He drew her close, swaying with her in the moonlight, and as their lips finally met, she knew the truth in her mother's words. *The dance was setting her free.*

Camilla's breath trembled as the last sparkles rose from the lake and vanished into the night. Her mother's reflection had already faded, but the ache of recognition lingered in her chest. She pressed her palm there, afraid to move, afraid the moment might dissolve if she did.

Without asking, Johnny stepped in behind her, his body warm against her back, his arms sliding around her waist. He said nothing—didn't question her sudden stillness, didn't pry into the mystery in her eyes. He simply held her, guiding her gently away from the railing until she was facing him.

The night music still floated from the street below, faint but rhythmic, as though the world itself was keeping time for them. Johnny caught her hand, his fingers threading through hers, and with the other hand, he cupped the curve of her back. Slowly, deliberately, he led her into a dance—sensual, unhurried, his steps a quiet invitation.

Camilla let herself be pulled into the rhythm, her cheek brushing against his as their bodies moved together. His breath was warm against her temple, his lips grazing the edge of her hair as though the dance itself demanded more than steps—it demanded closeness.

She closed her eyes and let the world blur, let her body answer his subtle guidance. Each sway, each turn deepened the connection until it felt less like dancing and more like surrender. When he finally tilted her face up to his, their lips found each other, the kiss soft at first, then lingering—passionate without haste, like music stretched into forever.

For Camilla, the bridge, the lake, even her mother's reflection all fell away. There was only the dance. Only Johnny. Only freedom.

Her lips still tingled from Johnny's kiss; her body still swayed to music that had already faded into the night. In that single heartbeat of silence afterward, Camilla knew nothing would ever be the same again.

# CHAPTER 39

The next morning, Charles rose earlier than usual, his sleep fractured by restless thoughts and a gnawing sense of things slipping beyond his control. The house was silent, the kind of silence that unsettled him, it was not the quiet of peace but the quiet of secrets.

Camilla's door was closed. He paused outside, listening, wondering if she was still asleep—or pretending to be. For a moment he thought of knocking, but instead he turned away and walked briskly down the hall, convincing himself he had more pressing matters.

# CHAPTER 40

At the bank, the atmosphere was tense but deceptively calm. Charles adjusted his tie, preparing to face another day of scrutiny, while in the shadows, Michael was already moving the pieces of his own scheme forward. Charles entered the bank through the marble vestibule with his usual stiff gait, but his confidence was a mask stretched too thin. His jaw clenched as he greeted employees with his customary nod. Their eyes followed him—not with respect anymore, but with suspicion. He felt it. He knew it.

The gray-suited agents had left, but their presence clung to the walls like smoke. Whispers followed him into the elevator; whispers he pretended not to hear.

Inside his office, Charles lowered himself into the leather chair, staring at the stack of papers Michael had left artfully arranged on his desk. "Compliance reviews," the cover sheet read. Charles tapped it with a single finger. He didn't need to open the folder. He knew what it contained—half-truths, clever diversions, and just enough falsified assurances to buy them time.

The intercom buzzed. "Mr. Huntington," Sylvia's voice came through, "Mr. Smithers is on line two. He says it's urgent."

Michael again. Charles's temples throbbed. The man had become both indispensable and intolerable—always with a smile too confident, always with answers too quick. He pressed the button anyway.

"Charles, old boy!" Michael's voice boomed as though they were still at the luncheon with Raptnor, as though the last two weeks hadn't nearly gutted their entire operation. "I've smoothed things over. You'll see—it's already working."

Charles pinched the bridge of his nose. "And by smoothed over, you mean what exactly?"

Michael chuckled. "Let's just say... loose ends are being tied. You'll have nothing to worry about soon."

Charles froze. The tone wasn't lost on him—nor was the deliberate vagueness. His gut tightened. Loose ends. He thought instantly of Camilla. The sudden fear that Michael's "solutions" extended into his private life made bile rise in his throat.

"You keep my daughter out of this," Charles said, his voice sharper than he intended.

"Oh, relax," Michael replied smoothly. "I'm just protecting our interests. And yours. You'll thank me one day."

The line went dead.

Charles sat in silence, staring at the skyline outside his window. Fifteen years ago, Raptnor had told him principles didn't pay for penthouses. He'd taken that lesson to heart. But now, with Michael moving pieces in shadows, Charles felt the walls of that gilded cage closing in tighter.

For the first time in years, he wondered if he'd traded too much.

# CHAPTER 41

The hum of the bank's air-conditioning filled the silence as Charles sat at his desk, his Scotch glass untouched.

The door opened without a knock. Michael strode in with his usual swagger, his silk tie slightly loosened, as if he owned the building rather than managed it. He dropped a slim folder on Charles's desk with a heavy thud.

"What's this?" Charles asked, eyes narrowing.

"Evidence," Michael said smoothly, lowering himself into the armchair opposite. "A tidy little package for compliance to review. Looks clean enough to close any lingering doubts."

Charles flipped the folder open. Inside were neatly typed statements, falsified dates, and forged client signatures—immaculate, impossible to dispute at a glance. His stomach churned. "You think this will hold?" Charles asked.

Michael grinned. "It doesn't need to hold forever. Just long enough for Raptnor's people to calm down and the regulators to move on to the next fire."

Charles shut the folder and leaned back, his knuckles white around the glass in his hand. "And what about the other matter you hinted at? My daughter?"

Michael waved dismissively. "Handled. Or it will be. Some little artist boy from the wrong side of town—he's not going to be a problem much longer."

Charles slammed the glass onto his desk, amber liquid sloshing over the rim. "I told you not to touch her!"

Michael's smile didn't falter. If anything, it deepened. "And I told you, I'm protecting the both of us. She's a liability, Charles. If anyone connects her with that boy, and if that boy starts digging where he doesn't belong..." He spread his hands, shrugging. "We lose everything. I'm making sure she doesn't drag us down with her."

The words lodged in Charles's chest like a stone. He wanted to hurl the folder at Michael, to shout him out of the office. But a darker fear gnawed at him—Michael was right. Camilla's secret life had become dangerous, not just for her but for him too.

Michael leaned forward, voice low and coaxing. "Trust me, Charles. You've always trusted me when the stakes were highest. Haven't I delivered before?"

Charles said nothing. He looked out the window instead, his reflection staring back at him in the glass. He saw a man cornered, a man who had long ago traded his soul for security and was now paying the price.

Michael rose, straightening his jacket. "Good. Then let me do what needs to be done." He left the office, the echo of the door clicking shut far too loud in the silence that followed.

Charles stared at the folder on his desk. It looked harmless enough, but he knew—inside those pages were lies that bound him to Michael tighter than chains.

For the first time, he wondered: was Michael protecting him... or burying him alive?

# CHAPTER 42

Nestling against Johnny's chest, Camilla traced idle patterns across his skin while staring at the ceiling. The antique candelabra cast honeyed light across the white plaster, shadows flickering and bending as though dancing to some secret tune. The loft smelled of oil paint, wood smoke, and the faintest sweetness from the flowers lining the sill.

Her gaze drifted to the corner where Lazlo's carefully wrapped book sat atop her folded clothes on the chair. For a moment, her stomach tightened—the reminder of clocks, consequences, and fathers who counted her steps more carefully than she dared admit.

Johnny's fingers slipped through her hair, calming the churn of her thoughts.

"Your father won't even notice. It's earlier than you think."

Her head lifted, eyes searching his. "How did you know what I was thinking?"

A lazy grin curved his lips. "I told you before. I know you." His thumb brushed over her temple.

The tension in her body dissolved. She pressed herself closer, her lips brushing the hollow of his throat. "Tonight has been perfect. You've been perfect."

"Then don't leave," he whispered, his breath warm against her ear as he shifted, rolling her gently beneath him. "I'm not nearly done with you."

Their laughter mingled with sighs as they found each other again, tender and fierce all at once. Her hands tangled in his hair, his traced the familiar map of her body with reverence, until movement became rhythm—until rhythm became something beyond either of them.

When finally they stilled, breathless, their bodies slick with warmth, Camilla lay curled against him, her cheek on his chest, listening to the steady drum of his heartbeat. She felt as though she had crossed a threshold she hadn't known existed—one she could never retreat from.

Johnny kissed the crown of her head, lingering there. "Do you feel it now?"

"Feel what?" she murmured.

"That you're alive," he whispered.

She closed her eyes, holding the words inside her as though they were the only truth that mattered.

# CHAPTER 43

It was just after six a.m., when Camilla slipped out of the taxi and padded softly up the front steps. The Huntington house loomed in its usual silence, but tonight the silence felt dangerous. Her key trembled in her hand. She was already rehearsing excuses—library study, late-night essay research—anything that might explain her absence if her father confronted her.

Johnny's voice whispered in her memory, steadying her: *"Keep the thought of our day together, our night."*

A smile tugged at her lips. *It was worth it. Whatever happens, it was worth it.*

The lock clicked softly, and she eased the door open. The hallway was still, hushed, the grandfather clock's pendulum the only sound. With measured steps, she tiptoed up the stairs, into her room, and shut the door behind her. Clothes fell to the floor in a quiet heap; she slipped into her nightgown and dove beneath her quilt, pulling it over her head. A girlish giggle escaped her lips. *Oh gosh, I can't believe it! Any of it!*

Sleep came quickly, deep and sweet.

The shrill ring of the telephone shattered it. Muffled voices floated from the hallway:

"Good morning, Señor Huntington, would you like a full breakfast this a.m.?" Paola's familiar voice.

"No, Paola," her father's sharp reply. "I've been at work all night. I just came home to shower. Hot coffee in a thermos—I need to be back in the limo immediately. If my daughter wakes, tell her I'm sorry I missed her."

Camilla buried her face in the pillow, heart racing. *He doesn't even know I was gone.* Relief bubbled up, almost laughter. *Yippee.*

She dozed again until the telephone jarred her awake once more. Groggy, she lifted the receiver.

"Jules, I'm too tired for breakfast," she mumbled.

But the voice on the other end wasn't Julie's. It was rough, almost mocking.

"Excuse me, this ain't Julie. Am I speaking to Camilla Huntington?"

Her spine stiffened. "Yes. Who is this?"

"Well hello sweet cheeks!, Name's Jimmy. Jimmy Pignato. Friend of your uncle Michael."

Confusion sharpened into annoyance. "Don't call me *sweet cheeks.* I don't know you. What do you want?"

"Relax, doll. I got the idea you liked bad boys and Jimmy is a bad boy. So how about it you and me?" Jimmy said assumption in his voice

"what the hell are you talking about?" Camilla blurted out

"No offense meant. Let's just say I did your uncle a little favor. Helped your daddy with a problem down in your boy's neighborhood." Jimmy told her the story

Her breath caught. "What problem?"

"Aw, come on. Don't play dumb. I offered your Johnny a sweet little deal. Cash the check, walk away from the uptown girl. You."

Jimmy chuckled low. "Easy money. But hey, Johnny wasn't biting. I'll give him that."

Camilla gripped the phone so tightly her knuckles whitened. *Johnny... the check...*

Questions swirled. *How did they know? Who else knows?* And one name flashed into her mind: Julie.

She slammed down the phone and immediately dialed her best friend. No answer. She typed a quick text: *Need to meet this morning. Call me.*

Seconds later, her phone trilled with Julie's special ringtone.

"Hey Cammy," Julie chirped.

Camilla's voice came out clipped. "Hi Julie. This is Camilla."

"Uh, yeah. I know. What's with the Sunday school voice? What's going on?"

"Nothing. We were supposed to meet. Are you ready?"

"Sure. Where to? That little coffee shop downtown?"

"No!" The word burst out louder than she intended. She lowered her voice. "No. Charmaine's Café. One hour."

Julie hesitated. "Cammy, are you sure you're all right?"

"Yes. I'm fine. See you soon."

She hung up before Julie could press further, her hand trembling as she set the receiver back in its cradle. The walls of her pristine room seemed to lean inward. Somewhere between fear and fury, she whispered, "What have you done, Daddy?"

# CHAPTER 44

Charmaine's Café was a cozy, slightly old-fashioned place tucked on a side street, smelling of butter, cinnamon, and fresh-brewed coffee. Camilla slipped into a booth by the window, her scarf pulled tight around her neck, trying to still the tremor in her hands. She kept glancing at the door, impatient for Julie's blonde hair and easy smile to appear.

Julie breezed in a few minutes later, tall and radiant despite her casual jeans and oversized sweater. She spotted Camilla instantly and waved, but her smile faltered when she saw the tightness in her friend's face. Sliding into the booth across from her, Julie leaned forward.

"Okay, spill it. You've got that look, Cammy—the one that says the world is ending."

Camilla forced a breath. "Jules… something happened this morning. I got a phone call. From someone named Jimmy. He said he was… working for Michael."

Julie's brows furrowed. "Michael? As in your dad's shadow-in-a-suit Michael?"

Camilla nodded, her throat tight. "Yes. This Jimmy told me that my father—and Michael—sent him to make Johnny go away. He offered him a check. A large check."

Julie's eyes widened. "You mean, like… a payoff?"

"Yes." Camilla's voice broke on the word. "They want him to disappear from my life. And this Jimmy—he said Johnny refused, but

Jules... what if he doesn't next time? Or what if they make him? What if they hurt him?"

Julie reached across the table, grabbing Camilla's trembling hands. "Cammy, listen to me. If Johnny refused, it means he's not going to sell out. And as for threats, we'll figure that part out. But I need you to be straight with me—did you tell anyone else about Johnny?"

Camilla shook her head no and then turned it suspiciously at Juli. "No one. Only you. You're the only one who knows."

Julie leaned back, lips pursed. "Then Michael's goons are watching you. That's how they know. They're not getting information from me, Cammy—you have to believe that."

"I do." Camilla's eyes brimmed, her voice dropping to a whisper. "But I'm scared, Jules. I feel like my father's shadow is everywhere. He can't just let me live. Even now, even after last night, I feel like he's already trying to take it all away."

Julie's blue eyes softened. "Cammy, listen. You're not a prisoner. And if your father thinks he can scare off the people you love, then he doesn't know you as well as I do. You're stronger than that. We'll figure out a way to protect Johnny. And you."

The waitress came by with two mugs, setting them down with a bright smile, oblivious to the storm swirling inside the booth. Camilla gripped hers with both hands, letting the heat steady her.

"I don't know what to do," she admitted. "If Johnny knew how dangerous Michael was—he might... he might leave me, Jules. Just to keep me safe."

"Then don't let him decide for you," Julie said firmly. "You love him, don't you? Then you fight. We'll outsmart your father and his pet vulture. But you have to tell Johnny what's happening."

Camilla stared into the steam rising from her cup, hearing her mother's voice again: *Let the dance set you free.* But what if the dance ended in ruin?

Julie squeezed her hand again. "Cammy... no more secrets. Not between you and Johnny. That's how they win. That's how your father wins."

Camilla swallowed hard, her heart pounding. "You're right. Tonight—I'll tell him tonight."

# CHAPTER 45

The air outside Charmaine's Café was sharp, biting through her sweater and scarf, but Camilla welcomed the sting. It grounded her. She let Julie's words circle in her mind—*no more secrets... tell Johnny tonight.* Yet each step along the damp cobblestones made her chest heavier.

She drifted aimlessly, letting her boots click softly against the sidewalk, her fingers brushing the cold iron railings that lined the street. A chill wind rustled through the plane trees overhead, their leaves scattering like whispers across the pavement. She pulled her scarf tighter, trying to keep out the cold but also the thoughts pressing in on her.

Every shadow felt like a pair of eyes, every footstep behind her made her heart quicken. Michael's presence—his influence—seemed to cling to the city itself, lurking in doorways and alleyways. *If they're watching me, then they're watching Johnny.*

Camilla paused on a small bridge over the narrow canal that cut through the quarter. The water reflected a dull gray sky, rippling faintly with the wind. She leaned over the railing, staring into its shifting surface, wishing she could see her mother's face again—just for strength. But only her own pale reflection looked back, eyes wide with doubt.

When she finally reached home, her courage waned at the sight of the great Huntington estate rising in solemn silence before her. The stone façade seemed harsher than ever, each window like a judge's eye, unblinking. She slipped her key into the heavy oak door and stepped inside, greeted by the faint smell of polished wood and roses from the housekeeper's arrangements.

The hallway was quiet—eerily so. Her father was gone, or so she thought. The silence gave her no comfort. Instead, it felt like the air before a storm, charged and waiting.

She hurried upstairs, closing her bedroom door behind her, and leaned against it, willing her heartbeat to slow. For a moment, she thought she was safe. Then she noticed the envelope sitting neatly on her writing desk, cream-colored with her name scrawled across the front in her father's bold, unmistakable hand.

Her fingers trembled as she reached for it, uncertain if it would hold another command, another threat, or something far worse.

Camilla slid a finger under the flap of the envelope and carefully unfolded the thick paper inside. The handwriting was unmistakably her father's—broad, deliberate strokes that usually carried the weight of instructions, not sentiment.

But tonight, the words startled her.

**My Dearest Camilla,**

I know I have not been present as I should be. My duties, my worries, and my pride have often stood between us. For that, I am deeply sorry.

The truth is that these last few weeks have been difficult. More difficult than I care to admit. And in the days ahead, they may grow harder still. In that time, I will need you beside me—not as my daughter who must obey, but simply as my daughter who believes in me.

Stand by me, Camilla. I cannot do this alone.

Whatever else may come, know that you are my greatest treasure. I may not say it often, but I am proud of you, and I need you now more than ever.

Your father,

Charles

Camilla sat down on the edge of her bed, the letter trembling in her hands. Never had she read such words from him. No demands, no corrections, no criticism—just an admission of need, a plea.

Her heart twisted. For a moment, the girl in her wanted to rush to him, to be the daughter he asked for. But another part of her—the woman who had tasted freedom, love, and belonging in Johnny's world—hesitated.

She folded the letter carefully and placed it back in the envelope. Then, curling up on her bed with the wrapped package from Lazlo still at her side, she whispered into the quiet room:

"I can't lose myself again... not even for you, Father."

# CHAPTER 46

Camilla sat for a long while with her father's letter in her lap, her mind caught between the ache of his plea and the warm echo of Johnny's laughter in her heart. She could hear both voices—the stern but trembling request of Charles, and Johnny's steady, certain tone: *"I know you. I see you."*

The thought struck her like lightning: *I need to talk to Johnny.*

She pushed herself up from the bed and moved to the mirror. Her reflection looked pale, conflicted, too much of her father's daughter in the somber nightgown she had just pulled on. Without hesitation, she slipped back into her skirt and blouse from earlier that day, then wrapped Johnny's gifted scarf snugly around her neck. The multicolored silk whispered its own reassurance, like her mother's voice carried in fabric.

She glanced once more at the letter on her desk. "I'll stand by you in my own way, Father," she whispered. "But I need to know what *my way* is first."

The house was quiet, the early morning chill seeping through the tall windows. Camilla tiptoed down the staircase, avoiding the step she knew would creak, and slipped out into the still-sleeping world.

The streets were damp with dew, lamps throwing soft halos in the mist. She walked quickly, boots clicking against the cobblestones, until she reached the familiar winding stairwell leading up to Johnny's loft. Her heart pounded—not from the climb, but from anticipation.

She paused at the landing, her hand on the iron railing, and whispered to herself, "He'll understand. He always does." Then, with a steady breath, she lifted her hand and knocked.

But when she knocked, silence greeted her.

She waited, pressing her ear to the door. No sound of footsteps, no faint scrape of brush against canvas, no hum of his familiar, careless tune. Only silence.

Her pulse quickened. "Johnny?" she called softly, and then again, slightly louder. Nothing.

Her hand fell to the knob, but it didn't turn. That was when she saw it—taped neatly to the doorframe, a scrap of paper with his scrawled handwriting:

*C –*

*had to run out, catch you later.*

*J.*

She blinked at the note, her lips parting in confusion. "But... I was suppose to pose tonight, he was expecting me?" she whispered out loud to no one

 Something about the briskness of the words unsettled her. He had never been curt with her before. No warmth, no flourish, not even her full name. Just "C."

Clutching the slip of paper between her fingers, she sank onto the cold stairwell step, the ironwork curling above her like shadows of vines. A strange emptiness pressed against her chest.

Had something happened? Was he avoiding her? Or was she imagining meaning where there was none?

The only answer was the faint rustle of the paper in her hand and the echo of her father's letter still tucked in her coat pocket. For the first time, the two worlds—Johnny's and her father's—seemed to pull at her in equal measure.

She folded the note carefully, slipped it into her scarf, and whispered, "Later, then." But the unease lingered.

# CHAPTER 47

Earlier that morning, Johnny had awoken with a start, the warmth of the bed still clinging to him. For an instant he thought Camilla was there, curled against him. But when he reached across the sheets, only emptiness remained.

"Camilla," he whispered into the silence.

A knock jarred him. "Johnny, open up, man! You in there?" Joey's voice was insistent.

Reluctantly, Johnny pulled on sweatpants and shuffled to the door. Joey barreled in, talking a mile a minute about rehearsal, the stage, their set for that night. But before Johnny could answer, Mr. Hempshaw intercepted him at the bottom of the stairs.

"Where are you rushing, boy?" the old man asked, brows arched.

"To the club—we've got work before the show," Johnny replied.

"You're forgetting someone," Hempshaw said pointedly. "Your grandfather."

Johnny's heart sank. "Damn," he muttered. He'd promised Alban lunch. Joey rolled his eyes but relented.

"Go," Joey said. "But you owe me tonight."

Johnny nodded, already sprinting for his car.

# CHAPTER 48

The Ridgemont gleamed like a European villa, its gardens bright with autumn chrysanthemums and the air thick with birdsong. Inside, Nurse Paulson beamed at Johnny as though he were the sunshine itself.

"Johnny, you rascal," she teased. "You and your grandfather are the only gentlemen left in this place."

Alban McTavish appeared with that same mischievous spark Johnny adored. Even bent with age, he carried himself like a Highland lord.

"You know where to take me, lad," Alban said, and Johnny laughed. Of course he did.

They pulled up to the corner where Hamish McDougal's food cart leaned beneath the pale afternoon sun, its metal sides glinting like a weathered sentinel. Steam rose from the hatch in slow, curling ribbons, carrying the smell of pepper, roasted meat, and flaky pastry through the cool air.

"Afternoon, Hamish," Alban called, stepping out and adjusting his scarf. "Still manning the post, I see."

Hamish squinted, his face creasing into a grin. "Aye and look who's escaped the palace! Shouldn't you be back at that fancy home of yours, takin' tea with the widows?"

Alban chuckled, slipping his hands into his coat pockets. "They only serve cucumber sandwiches, Hamish. I needed real food—and better company."

"Ha! Company, is it?" Hamish's eyes twinkled. "You'll not find much refinement here, lad. Just grease and gossip."

"Exactly what I came for," Alban said, lowering his voice as he slipped a folded bill into Hamish's calloused palm. "And don't argue—it's a tip, not a bribe."

Hamish glanced down, his brow rising. "That's too generous by half."

"Think of it as a contribution to the cause," Alban said lightly. "Keeping civilization alive—one pie at a time."

Hamish barked a laugh and handed over the box and two steaming cups of coffee. "Aye, then take your rations and go before I change my mind."

Johnny took the load, the heat from the box warming his fingers as they walked toward the cemetery gates. The iron bars creaked open, sunlight spilling over the worn stones beyond. Between the drifting leaves and the quiet hum of the afternoon, it felt as though the world was watching them step into someplace sacred and still.

The cedar bench awaited them beneath whispering trees. Alban broke his pie slowly, savoring every bite.

"You know why I eat here?" he asked.

"Because you want to be close to them," Johnny answered.

Alban shook his head gently. "Because I want to remind myself death isn't an end, lad. Gravestones are like trees in a forest. You can let them be monsters... or angels."

Johnny studied his grandfather's weathered face, traced by laughter and loss, and felt the boy inside him stir. The boy who had once wept right here, demanding answers for why his parents had left him.

"Don't let your love turn to hate," Alban said softly, as if reading his thoughts. "Follow your passion, Johnny. That's the legacy they left you, whether you believe it or not."

Then, out of nowhere, Alban began to hum. His voice wavered but carried the melody of *Pure Imagination*, and Johnny couldn't help but smile.

Alban took his hand and gave it a squeeze, and for a moment the cemetery no longer felt heavy with stone but alive with promise.

Alban's voice softened as he began to hum, the melody meandering like a stream. Then, words followed—half-sung, half-spoken—an invitation to dream.

"*Come with me*," he said, his voice a little shaky but warm. "*Step into a world that lives only in your mind. If you dare to look closely, you'll see it—it's all there waiting. A place where anything is possible.*"

He tapped Johnny's chest lightly. "The spin of a brush, the stroke of a bow, a note that lingers in the air—these are the wheels that can turn your imagination into reality. The world you create will defy reason, but it will be yours."

Johnny's throat tightened as his grandfather's humming deepened, filling the quiet cemetery with something fragile but eternal. Alban smiled and added with a mischievous glint, he sang in a soft voice "*If you want to glimpse paradise, my boy, you don't need a ticket or a map. Just open your eyes. Look around. Whatever your heart longs for—you have the power to make it so.*"

Alban's voice drifted softly into the air, a half-hummed tune that seemed to settle over the gravestones like mist. Then, with a glimmer in his eyes, he began to speak—not as if reciting words, but as though he were opening a door to another world.

*"Come with me, Johnny. Step into the place your heart has always known but your eyes have yet to see. A world spun from thought, stitched together by color and sound, born of nothing but your own imagination."*

He let the pause linger, his hand pressing lightly against Johnny's chest. *"When the brush spins in your fingers... when a bow draws across the strings... when music catches in the air—you are no longer bound to this world. You create a new one. A place without rules, without limits. A place where reason cannot follow, but beauty always will."*

Johnny felt the weight of the words settle deep inside him, more eternal than stone.

Alban's voice lowered, nearly a whisper. *"And if ever you long for paradise, don't waste your years chasing it in men's fortunes or empty halls. Just look around you. See it in the colors of the leaves, the curve of a smile, the flame of your own art. Anything your soul dares to want—you already carry the power to bring it forth."*

The old man leaned back, humming the refrain again. To Johnny it sounded less like a song and more like a spell, the kind that weaves itself into your marrow and never lets go.

Johnny drifted back to when he was thirteen years old and standing near this very bench, anger welling up inside and tears streaming down his face as he turned to a much younger Alban.

"Why did they do it? Why did they leave me, Grandfather? It's not fair, it's not fair!" young Johnny cried into his grandfather's black funeral suit.

"Johnny, my boy, listen to me. I could tell you all about how life is not fair... blah, blah, cliché after cliché... but I am not going to. I am going to give it to you straight and give you the answers. Your parents, my daughter and son-in-law, got caught up in the material world. They both became greedy, obsessed with the world of gold, diamonds, and money. With all those possessions came the seedy side of affluence: alcohol, drugs, parties, and doing whatever they could to have it all, no matter how selfish. But how lucky you are that they loved you enough to leave you a legacy!"

"Loved me! What are you talking about? Their car went off a bridge because they were drunk and reckless. Do you believe they were thinking of me when they hit that cold water, or their own immortality?" Johnny was channeling his inner adult.

His grandfather thought it was an astute observation coming from a thirteen-year-old. "Yes, they did a lot wrong. They were selfish and materialistic, and they were not generous with you with money or gifts, right?"

"Yes." Johnny was curious where this was going.

"The one thing they were always there for, no matter what they were doing—for what did they always make time? For what did they always have money?"

"My art?" young Johnny asked.

"Yes. They knew that your artistic ability, your love of color, music, and dance was and is your way out. That is why they left you on a path out. They left you with the ability to love deeply, Johnny, to see into the souls of those you paint, to learn and communicate through your talent. Don't let your love turn to hate. Follow your passion. Not for fame or power but for happiness. Do you understand?" And watching the change in young Johnny's face, his grandfather knew he would be ok.

Alban leaned back, his voice drifting into a low hum, words that seemed more a spell than a song.

*"Come with me, Johnny. Step into the place your heart has always known but your eyes have yet to see. A world spun from thought, stitched together by color and sound, born of nothing but your own imagination.*

When the brush spins in your fingers… when a bow draws across the strings… when music catches in the air—you are no longer bound to this world. You create a new one. A place without rules, without limits. A place where reason cannot follow, but beauty always will.

*And if ever you long for paradise, don't waste your years chasing it in men's fortunes or empty halls. Just look around you. See it in the colors of the leaves, the curve of a smile, the flame of your own art. Anything your soul dares to want—you already carry the power to bring it forth."*

The old man's humming returned, the rhythm slightly off-key, but the words still radiant. To Johnny it sounded less like a melody and more like truth, the kind that weaves itself into your marrow and never lets go.

The old man's humming faded into silence, leaving only the rustle of leaves and the hush of the cemetery air. Johnny sat still, his grandfather's words swirling through him like paint mixing on a palette.

Alban leaned forward, his hand resting on Johnny's knee. His voice was gentler now, but no less firm.

"Johnny, my boy, I don't remind you of these things for nostalgia's sake. Your gift isn't meant to be locked away. It was given to you for a purpose. And now, that purpose calls."

Johnny tilted his head, sensing the shift. "What do you mean?"

"Grandfather," Johnny said at last, "what do you need?"

"There is a man, a dear friend of mine—Milosh. You know him. The scarf you wear so often, he gave it to you." Alban's eyes clouded with sorrow Johnny had rarely seen. "He is fading, Johnny. Both in body and in spirit. And before he goes, he longs for something only you can give him: a memory made whole again."

"I need you to paint Milosh's daughter," Alban said. His eyes clouded. "My friend Milosh's daughter. She's gone, but he clings to her. He needs this. And soon."

Johnny felt his chest tighten. "Milosh's daughter... but she's gone."

"Yes," Alban said quietly, "but her image lives still. In photographs, in memory, in the trembling hands of a father who cannot let go. He needs her painted—not as she was at the end, but as she truly lived. He needs her light captured, so his heart may rest."

He gave me the last photograph he had of her.

Johnny nodded "Of course. Show me the picture. "and reached his hand out gently taking the old fragile photograph.

Johnny glanced at the gravestones surrounding them, the cold markers softened by his grandfather's words about angels and rebirth. The idea of giving someone back their daughter, if only in color and canvas, suddenly felt both immense and inevitable.

Alban placed his weathered hand over Johnny's. "This is not for fame, not for wealth. This is for love, and for healing. And that, my boy, is what your gift was always meant for."

Johnny swallowed hard, his mind already leaping ahead—to brushes, to hues, to the delicate lines of a face half-remembered. He nodded slowly. "Yes, Grandfather. I'll do it. I'll paint her."

The old man's smile returned, soft but proud. "Then you'll be giving him paradise, Johnny. And perhaps, without even knowing it, you'll be giving yourself a piece of it too."

Johnny lingered a moment longer on the cedar bench, his grandfather's words still humming in his ears. The breeze lifted fallen leaves across the path, like fragments of memory trying to take flight. He stood, steadying Alban with one arm, and together they walked out through the rusted iron gate.

The Porsche gleamed faintly under the muted sky as Johnny opened the passenger door and helped his grandfather inside. Neither spoke much on the ride back; silence itself seemed reverent, as if they were both carrying something delicate that couldn't be spoken aloud yet.

At Ridgemont, Johnny made sure Alban was settled back in his apartment with a cup of tea and Nurse Paulson hovering happily. "Next week, Johnny," his grandfather said, holding his hand firmly. "Bring me news of the painting."

"I will," Johnny promised, pressing his grandfather's hand with a conviction that felt like an oath.

# CHAPTER 49

Johnny climbed the narrow stairwell to his loft, dusk stretching long shadows across the brick walls. He let himself in, tossing his coat over the couch, his mind fixed only on the task ahead. He didn't notice the note to Camilla still taped to the door.

The loft was quiet, faintly echoing with her laughter, the ghost of her music. On the worktable, brushes lay scattered like weary soldiers. Johnny reached into his pocket and drew out the worn photograph Alban had given him—the image of Milosh's daughter. Her smile was soft, secretive, as if she'd known something the camera could never hold.

He slipped the photograph between sheets of cardboard and placed it carefully in his drawer. His hand lingered on the handle. "Two promises," he murmured. "One to Milosh... and one to her."

The lamp on his worktable cast a golden halo over the blank canvas, as if it already knew what it would hold. Johnny stretched the linen tight, breathing in the mingled scents of turpentine, old wood, and coffee. He closed his eyes and waited—not for inspiration, but for the girl to rise in his mind, no longer a faded photograph but alive, dancing, laughing.

His fingers twitched for the brush, but he didn't lift it. Some paintings demanded more than skill; they asked for reverence. He sat in the stillness, feeling the weight of love, grief, and the fragile bridge between the living and the dead—waiting until he was ready to begin.

At the same time, Camilla climbed the narrow staircase two at a time, her scarf pulled tightly against the cold. Her heart was beating faster with each step—

She had rehearsed what she would say to Johnny a dozen times on the way over—how she needed his advice, his truth, his way of seeing the world

When she reached his door, her hand trembled against the wood. She knocked once, twice. No answer.

Leaning closer, she spotted a scrap of cardboard taped neatly to the door:

*C – had to run out. Catch you later. J.*

Her chest tightened. Just four words, so casual, but they hit her like a lock snapping shut. She pressed her palm flat against the door as if she could reach through to him.

Johnny lit another lamp, adjusting the angle so the canvas glowed brighter. He reached for a brush but hesitated again, hearing his grandfather's voice in his head: *"Don't let your love turn to hate. Follow your passion... not for fame or power but for happiness."*

The words felt heavy, binding him to the promise he'd made. He dipped the brush in the paint, then stopped. Somewhere beneath the floorboards, he thought he heard faint footsteps retreating down the stairwell.

Camilla turned from the door, her scarf slipping loose around her shoulders. The note still burned in her hand. She walked slowly back down the stairs, her boots echoing in the narrow hall. A dozen questions tangled in her chest. *Why didn't he wait? Where did he go? Is he alright? What if my uncle, jimmy...?*

The city lights through the cracked windows looked blurry through the tears she didn't want to admit were forming. She clutched the note in her fist. "Later," it said. "ok later" she thought it will be ok her other thoughts were just her overemotional state at this point.

Johnny returned to his work, fully absorbed in his mission—so deep in concentration that the world beyond his canvas ceased to exist. When a knock sounded at the door, he didn't notice. It grew louder, more insistent, until the persistent rhythm finally broke through his focus.

He quickly answered thinking it might be Camilla but instead he was greeted by his friend Joey.

"Hey man what are you doing? You promised when you came back you would come to the club and help with the background mural and I am holding you to it!" Joey blurted out

Johnny tried to argue "but..."

"no buts a promise is a promise man.  Now grab your coat let's go"

Joey escorted Johnny out the door before he knew what was happening.

# CHAPTER 50

The club pulsed with restless energy. Colored lights splashed across the stage in shifting blues and purples as Joey and the others hauled planks of wood, hammered joints, and tested rigging. The tang of sawdust and spilled beer lingered in the air, mixing with the faint electric burn of stage equipment warming up. Johnny rolled up his sleeves, threw himself into the work, and forced himself not to think about the note taped to his loft door.

"Johnny, grab that end!" Joey barked, pointing to a heavy backdrop frame. Together they lifted it, sweat already soaking through their shirts. Johnny moved quickly, hands strong, mind disciplined. Yet each time he straightened, the image of Camilla—standing in his doorway, scarf pulled tight, eyes searching—flashed before him.

"Hey man, focus," Joey warned. "This gig could set us up for months. We need it perfect."

Johnny nodded, shoving Camilla's image to the back of his mind. But inside, guilt gnawed at him.

The backdrop rose into place, and Joey slapped Johnny on the back. "Perfect! We'll be ready by curtain tomorrow."

Johnny forced a smile, but his eyes drifted to the far corner where his canvas supplies waited in their bag. His grandfather's request, Camilla's expectant eyes, Joey's demands—the weight pressed on him from every side.

As the amps hummed to life and guitars struck their first distorted chords, Johnny shut his eyes for a moment, whispering to himself:

"One night. Just one more night to hold it all together."

# CHAPTER 51

Across town, Huntington Estate

Camilla sat cross-legged on her bed, Lazlo's book on her lap, unopened. She kept staring at the curt scrawl Johnny had left on the note: *C – had to run out. Catch you later. J.*

Her father's letter lay open beside her, the words echoing like a plea: *I will need you in the coming weeks… please stand by and support me.* The contradiction twisted her heart—one man calling her closer, another pushing her away.

The silence of her room pressed in. For the first time, she dialed Julie without hesitation.

"Cammy? You sound… strange."

"Julie… can we meet tonight? Please? I just—I need someone to talk to."

Charmaine's Café glowed with soft amber light, the clink of porcelain cups and the low hum of conversation filling the air. Julie spotted Camilla immediately—her scarf pulled tightly around her shoulders, her expression far away. She waved her over, already reading the signs.

"You've got that look again," Julie said as soon as Camilla sat down. "The one that says you're hiding something."

Camilla stirred her coffee without tasting it, eyes fixed on the swirling cream. "Julie... you know that man that called me and said he offered me money?"

Julie's eyes widened. "Did he call again!—"

"No it's just I remember he told me Johnny has the check. Johnny hasn't told me." Camilla's voice trembled, a mix of anger and fear. "Why wouldn't he tell me?"

Julie leaned forward, her tone urgent. "Cammy, listen. Men do dumb things when they think they're protecting you. Maybe he didn't want to worry you. But you have to ask him directly."

"We were suppose to see each other tonight, posing as usual, but when I went to the loft he wasn't home this note was taped to the door" Camilla handed Julie the note

Julie read it and had a slight frown on her face and then smiled "Cammy this doesn't mean anything, at least he remembered to leave you a note. I know you two have been snug in your old little world, hiding away in his loft but there is another world out there and maybe he has other business, friends and commitments too"

Camilla looked down "yes your right, I only know his friend Joey maybe he had something else to do" her hands gripping the mug tightly. "But what if he *took it*? What if they were right about him all along?"

Julie squeezed her hand across the table. "Then you'll know the truth. But from what I've seen? He's not that guy."

# CHAPTER 52

Back at the club, the air was electric. The stage lights blazed as musicians tested microphones, guitars wailed in distorted warmups, and dancers rehearsed their steps at the edge of the floor. Johnny crouched on the stage, paintbrush in hand, finishing the bold swirls of color across the backdrop.

"Damn, Johnny, that's wild," Joey said, leaning over his shoulder. "Looks like fire and water collided."

Johnny grinned faintly, but his mind wasn't here. Every stroke of paint was haunted by Camilla's face, the way she'd leaned into him under the garden lights, the whisper of her mother's voice in her ears. He shoved the thought aside, telling himself he'd explain tomorrow. *She'll understand. She has to.*

The crowd outside the doors grew louder, laughter spilling into the night. The sound reminded Johnny of Giovanni's café, of Camilla's trembling hands on the violin strings. The contrast twisted something inside him.

The house lights dimmed, a hush falling over the crowd. Then a single spotlight ignited, illuminating the canvas that hung at the back of the stage. Gasps spread through the room, followed by a swell of applause.

Johnny stood just off to the side, paint still clinging to his hands, the scent of turpentine faint on his clothes. The piece was bold—sweeping strokes of crimson and indigo colliding in a storm of fire and water, light and shadow, chaos and serenity. It was a mirror of the world he carried inside him, the one he rarely let anyone see.

The applause grew louder, reverberating against the club's exposed brick walls. Joey clapped him on the back. "See? I told you they'd get it, Johnny. They *feel* it."

But Johnny only half-heard. His eyes lingered on the painting, yet his mind was with Camilla—her laughter, her bow across Giovanni's violin, the look in her eyes when she realized she belonged in that world of color and sound. That memory mattered more than any ovation.

The applause was still thundering when Johnny stepped back into the shadows of the club. Strangers clasped his hands, congratulated him, spoke of brilliance and vision. But even as their words washed over him, his eyes kept searching the crowd for someone who wasn't there.

A ripple of unease crept into him. Camilla should have been here why didn't I call her before I came out. He imagined her face tilted up toward the painting, her smile widening as she saw what he'd poured into it—how much of her lived in those strokes of crimson and blue. Instead, the space beside him was empty, and the echo of her laugh was nowhere to be found.

He clapped politely at Joey's jokes, but his chest tightened with a gnawing absence. Something was missing, something vital.

"You look distracted, man. Uptown girl got you whipped already?" Joey's voice dripped with sarcasm.

Johnny shot him a tired glance. "Drop it, Joey."

But his friend only smirked. "Just saying—you don't belong in her world. She'll wake up one day, realize you're just a starving artist, and she'll be gone. Better you learn that now than later."

Johnny clenched his jaw. "She's not like that."

# CHAPTER 53

At the café, Camilla rose abruptly, her chair scraping against the tile. "I can't sit here anymore. I need to know."

Julie stood too, steadying her friend. "Do you want me to come with you?"

Camilla shook her head. "No. I'm not going to chase after him like some crazed teenager. I just need to calm down and take the emotion out of it. I'm going home, running a hot bath, putting on some soft music, and getting a good night's sleep. Tomorrow, I'll surprise him with coffee and breakfast—he's always doing sweet things for me. I just need to trust what we have. Thanks, Jules. I'll call you tomorrow."

Jules gave Cammy a quick supportive hug and they both went on their way.

Camilla pulled her coat tighter and stepped into the night air, the city's lights flickering against her scarf. As she walked, her pulse quickened. Johnny's note, her father's letter, Jimmy's threat—all tangled together in her mind like a knot she didn't yet know how to unravel.

When she arrived, the Huntington house loomed tall and silent, but her father's letter still lay on her desk where she'd left it. She picked it up again, reading the words aloud in a whisper:

*"Please stand by me. I will need you in the coming weeks. I need my daughter."*

<h1 style="text-align:center">CHAPTER 54</h1>

Waking from a quick twenty-minute nap after being up all night, Johnny dragged himself upright, his body heavy with exhaustion. He rubbed his face, muttering, "Coffee. Strong coffee—that's the answer." Pulling on his coat over a pair of old sweats, he shuffled out into the cold air, the brisk wind shocking his senses awake as he made his way to the corner shop.

Maria, at the counter, beamed when he walked in. "Johnny," she said, tucking a strand of hair behind her ear, "double tired this morning, I can tell. I'll make it quick."

Normally, Johnny would've teased back with a wink, but today he only managed a distracted smile. His thoughts were already back at the loft, racing toward the unfinished painting. Maria's smile faltered, but she handed him the bag of beans anyway, watching him go.

By the time Johnny hurried back up the stairs, Camilla was waiting, arms full—two cups of steaming coffee and a tray of fresh pastries.

"Camilla?" He blinked at her, surprised. "What are you doing here?" His voice came out sharper than he intended, curt from fatigue.

She hesitated, then lifted the cups with a hopeful smile. "I thought I'd surprise you. Breakfast, for a change."

Something in Johnny softened. "Oh... sorry. I was out late last night. Sure, come on up."

They sat at the little table, steam rising between them. The pastries were sweet, the coffee hot, but the silence was heavy. Camilla fidgeted, then began gathering up the empty cups. Johnny reached across the table to stop her.

"No, don't. You've done enough already. I needed this, truly." He hesitated, then added, "But, Camilla... I'm buried today. Can we pick this up later? Tonight?"

Her face fell. "Of course. Tonight around seven?"

"Perfect." Johnny tried to smile, but his eyes kept darting toward the covered easel.

Camilla followed his gaze. "Great. Oh, but first—let me see the painting!" She rose quickly, excitement breaking through her unease.

In an instant, Johnny was in front of her, his voice booming. "NO!"

The word cracked like a whip. His face was pale, eyes wide.

Camilla stopped, trembling, her lips quivering. "If that's how you feel... maybe I should just leave altogether."

Johnny's expression collapsed into regret. He reached for her hand. "No, please. I'm sorry. I just—I need it to be perfect before you see it. That's all. Forgive me?" He leaned in and kissed her softly, trying to mend the fracture.

Against her better judgment, her heart melted. She nodded, whispering, "Okay."

"Good," he said, forcing a smile. "Why don't you warm up those pastries? I'll splash water on my face and then we'll talk." He kissed her forehead, then quickly lifted the canvas and carried it with him into the bedroom.

Camilla watched him, uneasy. Why so secretive? Was he painting someone else? A flicker of jealousy rose before she could stop it. *Don't be ridiculous,* she scolded herself. *You're not a jealous girl—just ask him later.* But the thought lingered, sharp and unwelcomed.

In the kitchen, she reheated the pastries, searching for a knife to spread the butter. Opening the drawer, she froze.

A check lay half-hidden among the utensils. The numbers leapt out at her—impossibly large. And the signature at the bottom: **her uncle's.**

Her stomach lurched. Her breath caught in her throat.

The pieces fell together in her mind with brutal clarity. Johnny's distraction, his secrecy, his sudden temper—it wasn't about art. It was about money. About her. About being bought and sold like a trinket in Lazlo's shop.

Tears blurred her vision as anger surged through her chest. She snatched her coat from the chair, bolted for the door, and slammed it behind her before he could emerge from the bedroom.

<h1 style="text-align:center">CHAPTER 55</h1>

The stairwell smelled of damp concrete and old varnish. Camilla's heels clattered against the worn steps as she half-walked, half-ran, the sound sharp in the silence. Each echo was another heartbeat, another tear threatening to spill.

*How could I be so stupid?* Her mind screamed at her as she pressed her hand to the cool metal railing. *I thought Johnny was different. I thought this—* she swallowed hard *—was real.*

The check's numbers burned into her memory, seared like an iron brand. And her uncle's signature—so unmistakable—mocked her.

*All this time... was it just about money? Was I just another Huntington payoff?*

Her throat tightened. She thought of his kiss on the bridge, the way he had held her, the way she had believed him when he told her she belonged.

*Lies. All of it. He said I belonged with him, and all along he was already being paid to let me go.*

The thought of the painting and how he secretly whisked it away from her. The painting wasn't of her? Who else was posing, did he do this with every woman he met?

By the time she reached the ground floor, her eyes were brimming. She shoved the door open, letting the cold air bite her cheeks. She didn't stop walking, her scarf tugged tight around her neck like armor.

The city blurred around her, people just shadows as she stormed down the street. In her chest, heartbreak and fury twisted together until she could barely breathe.

*I gave him everything... and just like every other man, he took what he wanted. And now he's bored.*

Her vision blurred with fresh tears, but her steps only quickened.

*Never again,* she vowed silently. *Never again will I let myself be fooled by promises or pretty words. If Johnny thinks I can be bought, if my own family thinks they can control me... they'll all find out just how wrong they are.*

# CHAPTER 56

Running up the street, cold wind biting her cheeks, Camilla whispered into the dark:

*"Mom, I miss you so much. This is a time when a girl really could use a mother to talk to."*

Shaking off her emotions, she thought of the most obvious answer—Google.

She darted past Paola, straight up the stairs, and into her room. The sleek computer on her ornate desk seemed almost foreign. A gift from her father for her studies was rarely used for anything more than emails. She preferred the library, where pages smelled of ink and dust, not electricity.

Tonight, though, it was the quickest tool she had.

Fingers trembling on the keyboard, she typed *John Oshay.* Before pressing enter, doubt hit her. *"What are you doing, Camilla? Acting like some paranoid millennial?"* She exhaled and hit return anyway.

The results were disheartening. No social media, no website, no obvious digital footprint. *Maybe the name is fake.*

Not ready to give up, she tried variations, searches that went nowhere. Then inspiration struck—Joey Marconie. Jackpot. Joey was plastered across Facebook: photos at the club, tagged friends, endless posts. And there, in the background, Johnny—smiling, alive, unposed, undeniably real.

But when she clicked on his tag, her hope deflated. The page was barren, inactive, almost like a ghost account.

Frustrated, she closed the tabs and wiped her history. *Fine. If the answers aren't here, I'll go old school - the library.*

Throwing on her coat and scarf, she stormed downstairs, intent on unraveling the truth herself.

# CHAPTER 57

Charles's limo slid to a halt in front of the bank. He straightened his tie, inhaled deeply, and

braced for the day's storm.

"Excuse me, are you Charles Huntington?" a crisp voice cut through the morning air.

Charles turned, irritation ready. "Yes, but you'll need to make an appoint—"

The stranger shoved an envelope into his hand. "You've been served." Without another word, the man strode away.

Charles's stomach plummeted. His worst fear—realized.

Inside his office minutes later, Sylvia was already on the phone to his attorney as Charles skimmed the accusations. Wire fraud. Money laundering. Ties to known felons.

The familiar scent of Michael's cologne struck him before the man himself appeared, waving his own copy of the summons.

"Did you see this?" Michael fumed. "The nerve, the gall! How can you just sit there?"

"Miles is on his way," Charles muttered, forcing calm. "We'll manage it."

"Manage it?" Michael hissed. "This could go public, Charles. The last thing you need is reporters digging into your daughter's... extracurriculars."

Charles bristled. "Leave Camilla out of this. We deal with the case. That's all." He slammed the intercom. "Sylvia! Get Raptnor on the phone."

# CHAPTER 58

Camilla rushed out of the house on the way to the library, coat trailing behind her, just as Charles stormed inside, papers clenched in his fist.

They collided in the hallway.

"Oh, Father—I'm sorry!"

He steadied her. "No, my dear. Are you hurt?"

She shook her head, then frowned. "Why are you home so early?"

"Nothing," Charles grumbled, stalking toward his study.

But Camilla followed. When she saw the court papers on his desk, her heart clenched. "Father... this looks serious."

"It is." His voice was grave.

And then his eyes flicked to her scarf. His temper snapped. "What is that around your neck?"

She startled, yanking it free. "It's nothing—just from... a friend. But it doesn't matter anymore."

"A boy?" His words cut like a knife.

"Yes. But I was mistaken about him. You don't have to worry—I won't see him again."

Charles studied her face, looking for the lie. He found none. Relief softened his expression. "Good. Because I need you now, Camilla. By my side. Firm. Strong."

She nodded, swallowing the ache in her chest. "Of course, Father. Whatever you need."

For a brief moment, the world shrank to just the two of them: a father fighting to hold onto his empire, and a daughter torn between duty and the ghost of a boy she couldn't forget.

# CHAPTER 59

Camilla sat at her vanity, smoothing foundation over the faint shadows beneath her eyes. The mirror reflected someone older than she felt—more solemn, more determined. Her father's note lay folded beside her brush set; the words etched into her like a brand: *"...will you please stand by and support me. I need my daughter."*

She inhaled sharply. Then that is what I will do. No more sneaking around, no more rebellions. I will be the daughter he wants me to be.

The resolve steadied her hands as she fastened her pearl earrings. But beneath the crisp blouse and perfect posture, her thoughts kept snagging on Johnny—on the way he had kissed her, on the secrets in his eyes, on the sting of his rejection.

*Why won't he just tell me the truth?*

Unable to stop herself, she picked up the phone and dialed Julie.

"Cammy? You sound... different," Julie answered cautiously.

"I need your help," Camilla said, her voice firm but threaded with desperation. "I'm going to stand with my father. That part is decided. But... I can't get Johnny out of my head. Something isn't right. I found something in his apartment, Julie. A check. From my uncle. And I don't know what it means."

There was a silence on the other end before Julie spoke again, softer. "Do you want me to look into him? Discreetly?"

"Yes." Camilla's grip tightened on the receiver. "Find out everything you can. I have to know who he really is. And if he's been lying to me. I tried looking him up on the internet, I found nothing he is a ghost"

"Don't worry go do what you have to do I got your back, let me look into this and then we can regroup, meet at the coffee shop." Julie said confidently

She hung up before her courage could falter, her heart split in two—one half claimed by duty to her father, the other chained to the boy who haunted her every breath.

# CHAPTER 60

Camilla slumped into the café booth across from Julie, her scarf trailing from her shoulders like a banner of surrender. Julie leaned in, eyes sharp.

As Julie started to tell her about her efforts to get information on Johnny she stopped noticing her friend was distracted and she did not have her full attention.

"Cammy, what's going on? You've been a ghost."

Camilla exhaled. "I don't have the mindset for Johnny right now. My father's in the fight of his life, and he needs me. I can't... split myself in two."

Julie reached for her hand. "I get it. But maybe talking to Johnny would help clear your head?"

Camilla hesitated, then pulled out her phone. The screen lit up with dozens of missed calls and unread messages—all from Johnny. She stared at them for a long beat, then shrugged and slid the phone face down on the table.

"I can't do this with him anymore," she said flatly. "Not now."

Julie opened her mouth to argue but stopped, recognizing the steel in her friend's voice. "Then you do what you have to do. Just... don't cut out your heart while you're saving your father."

Camilla gave her a small, grateful smile, but her eyes drifted to the window, her reflection split by the glass.

# CHAPTER 61

The next few weeks were among the hardest of Charles's life. Ordered to appear in Washington before a Senate subcommittee investigating the banks, he followed his attorney's advice and prepared a frank admission of fault and a sincere apology.

He arrived early. The auditorium was hushed, a bowl of tiered seating wrapped in dark wood. He found his name card, sat, and listened to his own breathing. One by one, people filtered in. Then Emmet Raptnor swept through the doors with a polished entourage—his VP of Marketing, his attorney, a perfectly turned-out PR executive. They moved as if this were routine, a calendar item between lunch and cocktails.

Charles approached, jaw tight. "This will be resolved, correct?"

Emmet's practiced smile never wavered. His lids drooped with ease. "A slap on the wrist, my boy. A slap on the wrist—I promise."

The morning blurred. Senators asked pointed questions; the Barclay team answered smoothly, their rhythm unbroken. Raptnor barely spoke. He sat with a faint grin while counsel and PR absorbed the blows and redirected them, ensuring the institution—and its thousands of employees—took the weight rather than the man at its pinnacle.

When Charles's name was called, he stood, palms damp. He'd rehearsed these pages so often he could have spoken them from memory, but he gripped his notes anyway. He greeted each committee member by title, then read:

"Esteemed committee members, Global Bank and Trust, of which I am the CEO, recognizes that our compliance has been unacceptable. We have learned hard lessons and are determined to do better. Rest assured, substantial steps are now in place to ensure this will never happen again."

He completed his apology with as much humility as he could summon. "Thank you for your time this morning and for allowing me to speak."

Relief loosened his chest—until the chairman replied.

"Thank you, Mr. Huntington. While we accept your apology and note your reforms, this does not change the fact that your bank—and you, as CEO—are responsible for knowing your customers and the origin of funds. When money is dirty, it is your duty to comply with the law. This is an investigative hearing only. Others, over whom we have no control, will take this further down the legal system. This committee is adjourned."

Color drained from Charles's face. He turned toward Raptnor's table just in time to see Emmet and his people rise and glide out without a word.

*When does this end? What happens next? Who are the "others"?*

# CHAPTER 62

Hundreds of miles from Washington's paneled chambers, Benjamin Silberman sat at a desk swallowed by folders. Thirty-five going on forty-five, he wore the weight of his work in fine lines at the corners of his eyes. Assistant district attorney. Respected. Tired.

He opened the top file. "Emmet Raptnor—refined, clever, fluent in the code. More difficult than anticipated."

The next: "Charles Huntington—ambitious, money-motivated, but small-town banker at heart. A pawn?"

And then: "Michael Smithers. A layup—except he was smart enough to push responsibility up the ladder."

Benjamin closed the last folder, a slow grin forming. *There's enough here to bring them to ground. Big-shot bankers are not above the law.*

Because of the banking nexus, his hands were tied to federal channels. He had drafted, redrafted, and sent the package to Justice two weeks ago, making sure there wasn't a comma out of place.

The phone rang.

"Benjamin Silberman," he answered.

"Mr. Silberman, Ms. Casey for Mr. Hubert, Assistant Attorney General, Criminal Division. Mr. Hubert would like you in Washington to meet with him and the U.S. Attorney for the Eastern District of New York as soon as possible. When can you fly?"

"I'll be on a plane tonight. Nine a.m. tomorrow."

"Noted."

He set down the receiver, pulse ticking faster. Months of preparation were about to step into the light.

# CHAPTER 63

Johnny paced, phone to his ear. "Camilla, it's Johnny again. Please call me We need to talk. You know where to find me." He ended the message, staring at the silent screen, then slid the phone facedown and turned to the easel.

Palette in one hand, brush in the other, he moved toward the half-finished portrait, then away. Something was wrong. The face was technically sound, the proportions exact—but the life wasn't there. Painting from a photograph always risked that: the likeness without the soul.

He lifted the worn snapshot from the easel's edge—Milosh's daughter, frozen in a moment from another life—and studied it as if it might answer back. "Who are you?" he asked softly. "What happened to you?"

A chill traced his spine, followed by an odd warmth, as if the image exhaled. A sensation bloomed inside him: *tragedy braided with joy.* It was contradictory, impossible—and undeniable.

He reached for fresh pigment. He reworked the eyes, deepening the lights, sinking the shadows, letting the irises glisten with a happiness that was undeniably real—and yet, beneath it, a seam of sorrow. He felt her love, and her loss, surge through his chest so fiercely he had to lower the brush and simply stand there, breathing with her.

Tears slipped free. This wasn't mere connection to a subject; it was as if the woman on the canvas had stepped into him and was looking out through his hands.

He steadied himself, looking from the painting to the photograph and back again. A familiarity stirred at the edges of his mind. He blinked, leaned closer—then froze.

"Oh my God."

# CHAPTER 64

Julie hustled down the sidewalk, a shopping bag in one hand, a box tucked under her arm, her phone open to a to-do list that refused to shrink. The screen lit with an unknown number. Decline. She reached the dry cleaner's door; the phone rang again. Decline.

"Clean and press all, please," she told the clerk.

"Ticket in a moment," the woman said cheerfully.

The phone rang for a third time. Same number. Julie almost hit decline again, then let it roll to voicemail. "Sales calls," she muttered to the clerk. "They never stop."

A chime announced the message. She pressed play, ready to block.

"Hello, Julie, this is Johnny. Johnny Oshay, a friend of Camilla's… I got your number from her. I haven't been able to reach her and it's urgent I speak with her. Could you call me, please? My number is— thank you."

Julie's brows lifted. *Well, well.* She tapped call back.

"Hello?" The voice was low, warm, and too earnest to be fake.

"Johnny? This is Julie—Camilla's friend."

"Thank you for calling. I—could you help me reach her? Or… would you talk with me? Please."

The reporter in her overruled the schedule. "Twenty minutes. The café on Birch."

"Perfect," he said, relief plain.

Twenty minutes later, Julie slid into a table and set down her packages. A presence stirred behind her.

"Julie?"

She turned—and momentarily forgot words. "Wowzer," slipped out before she could catch it.

"Excuse me?" Johnny laughed.

"Coffee," she recovered, grinning. "We should get coffee."

He ordered for them; the counter girl all but swooned. When he returned, Julie studied him frankly. "If Cammy told you anything about me, she probably mentioned I have no filter. So—yes, I see what she sees. Question is: are you as good underneath as the cover?"

"I hope so," he said simply. "I care for her. Very much. Whatever upset happened—it's worth fixing."

"Camilla runs at the first red flag," Julie said. "She learned that from a lifetime with a man who can't bend."

"Running is her thing," Johnny admitted, smiling despite himself. "So is bravery."

They talked for an hour—about Charles's legal mess, about money, art, neighborhoods, and loyalty—and always circling back to Camilla. Johnny's urgency wasn't performative; it pulsed through every word.

Julie stood to go. "Okay, Johnny-from-the-loft. Keep your phone on. I'll try to get her to listen."

He hugged her—solid, grateful. She surprised herself by hugging back.

Outside, Julie texted: *I'm coming over. Don't say no. Need to talk.* followed by a row of hearts and a kiss—because sometimes the only way to reach Cammy was to soften the landing.

# CHAPTER 65

Camilla's eyes stayed glued to the television screen, her breath shallow as her father approached the Senate podium. Under the harsh lights, Charles looked like a man ten years older—shoulders slumped, new streaks of gray curling at his temples, shadows carved under his eyes.

"Oh, Daddy... what did you get yourself into?" she whispered.

The camera panned as he began his prepared remarks, voice measured, every syllable deliberate. Camilla felt an odd rush of pride—he sounded strong, even noble. But when the committee chairman responded, the words cut through her hope like a blade.

"...Although we appreciate your apology... this does not change the fact that your bank, and you as CEO, are responsible. Others, I'm afraid, will take this further down the legal system."

Camilla slumped back on the couch. She didn't notice Julie until a hand squeezed her shoulder.

"Cammy."

"Oh—Jules!" Camilla blinked away her shock. "I didn't hear you come in."

Julie perched beside her, eyes flicking to the screen. "How's he holding up?"

Camilla managed a weak smile. "He just gave his speech. He... he did all right."

Julie waited, letting the silence settle before shifting the conversation. "And what about you? You holding up?"

Camilla exhaled. "I don't know. It's all too much. I can't even think about—" she stopped short, but Julie caught the hesitation.

"Johnny?" Julie pressed.

Camilla stiffened. "How can I think about him now? My father needs me."

Julie crossed her arms, tilting her head knowingly. "But don't you want to at least know the truth of what happened between you two?"

Camilla reached for her phone defensively. The screen lit up with a scroll of missed calls and unread messages—all from Johnny. Dozens. She shrugged with a hollow laugh. "See? He doesn't stop. I can't do this right now... maybe ever. I can't be pulled in two directions anymore."

Julie studied her friend's face and saw the sadness behind her bravado.

# CHAPTER 66

The hearing left Charles hollow. As the committee adjourned, senators shuffling papers and aides snapping briefcases shut, Charles lingered in his seat. His hands trembled around the edges of his statement, the carefully typed pages now crumpled and damp.

He had done what Miles, his attorney, told him—show contrition, admit fault, promise reform. But instead of mercy, he'd been served a warning: *others will take this further.*

*Others.* The word echoed.

In the hallway outside, cameras flashed. Reporters surged forward, microphones thrust like bayonets. Charles ducked his head, ignoring the barrage of questions. "Mr. Huntington! Did Global Bank knowingly launder money for criminal clients?" He pushed through the crowd, jaw clenched, coat collar raised like armor.

Emmet Raptnor and his team, however, glided past with ease. Their lawyer smiled broadly, tossing off a bland statement about "continued cooperation" while Raptnor adjusted his cufflinks, as though this was a game he'd already won.

Charles's stomach churned.

# CHAPTER 67

Back in the hotel suite, Charles sank into the leather armchair as though the weight of the world had dragged him there. Miles pressed a scotch into his hand, but Charles barely noticed.

"You did fine," Miles said, his voice practiced, professional. "The apology will look good on the news."

"Look good?" Charles rasped, staring into the amber liquid. His hand shook. "They said prosecution is inevitable."

Miles kept talking—something about politics, about posturing—but the words blurred. All Charles could hear was the word *inevitable*. His grip tightened until the glass cut into his palm.

"They'll make an example of you," Miles was saying.

Charles's heart hammered in his chest. His daughter's face rose before him—Camilla, laughing, carefree. The image split, darkened, became Viola. Lost Viola. The guilt welled up like bile.

"And my daughter?" he forced out, voice cracking. "What happens to Camilla if—"

But Miles's answer didn't matter. Charles's mind was already spiraling, his thoughts collapsing into the truth he could no longer hold back.

"You don't understand!" he shouted suddenly, the scotch sloshing over his hand. "You don't know what I've done—what I've traded—to climb this high. If I lose Camilla now, like I lost Viola... it's me. My fault. All of it!"

The sobs broke him then, laying waste on his chest, dragging him down. He bent forward, face buried in trembling hands, the years of ambition, greed, and compromise finally tearing open inside him.

## FLASHBACK

He saw Milosh again, as vividly as if he were standing in front of him. The modest home. The cobblestone path. The faint melody of a violin drifting from inside while the smell of cabbage and potatoes floated in the air.

Milosh's eyes had been full of disbelief, his voice ragged. *"You promised Viola a better life. You said we could keep our home. Why are you doing this?"*

Charles had stood there in his polished suit, a legal document in hand like a blade. His voice, back then, had been cold, resolved. *"I am taking care of her. Viola deserves a proper home. Respect. I need respect. Take the money—or take the eviction."*

Milosh's wife had wept openly in the doorway. With a forced smile meant to shield her, Milosh had signed. His voice, low, broken, had been a final plea. *"Give her comforts we cannot. But please—give her love. Let her keep her joy."*

The memory dissolved, leaving Charles hollow in the dim hotel suite. His glass sat untouched, the scotch now warm and lifeless.

He had not given Viola love. He had not given her joy. Only promises he had broken—and a legacy of sorrow that now threatened to claim his daughter as well.

# CHAPTER 68

The next month blurred for Camilla. She lived between two worlds—her father's collapsing empire and the aching distance from Johnny. Careful not to upset Charles further, she kept her head down, offering him quiet loyalty and patience. At night, though, when she couldn't sleep, she reached for her phone. She talked to Julie, who lent her a friends ear – and just listened and empathized.

Johnny waited. Camilla waited. Time moved like a slow fuse toward an explosion neither could predict.

Charles, however, felt no such stillness. For him, every day was another tick on the clock toward ruin. The hearings in Washington had cracked open the walls he built around his career. He lived with the suffocating dread of a man waiting for the axe to fall, knowing it was only a matter of when.

# CHAPTER 69

For Benjamin Silberman, the waiting was over. He knew it from the moment he walked into the Justice Department's pristine conference room. The place was immaculate—polished oak, matching drapes, antique trinkets in perfect symmetry. It reeked of order, control, and the kind of power that didn't get its hands dirty.

Benjamin had come prepared—briefcase stuffed with folders, months of late nights distilled into neat stacks of evidence. But the secretary, Ms. Casey, gently pushed the case aside, saying, "I don't believe paperwork will be necessary, Mr. Silberman. Mr. Hubert just wants to talk."

That was the first red flag.

Then Hubert entered, flanked by Mr. Crossly and Ms. Donaldson of the Eastern District Attorney General's office. Benjamin stood, eager, proud. At last, the system was going to act.

Instead, Hubert's words struck like a hammer:

"Mr. Silberman, thank you for your diligence. But we are asking you to stand down. Crossly and Donaldson will handle things from here."

Benjamin blinked, stunned. "But... surely you'll want my help indicting the executives? I've prepared this case for months—"

Hubert's tone was final, almost bored. "There will be no court case. A deferred prosecution, fines, oversight—these are the tools that protect the economy while correcting mistakes. You must understand—if we pursued full legal action, Barclay's U.S. charter would be revoked.

Thousands of jobs lost. Billions erased from the economy. That is not an acceptable outcome."

Benjamin's voice broke with fury. "Millions are dead because cartels moved money through these banks! And you call this oversight?"

Hubert's gaze didn't flicker. "You are not seeing the big picture. Thank you for your service, Mr. Silberman. Ms. Casey will handle your documents and NDA."

And with that, it was over. Months of work, sleepless nights, the perfect case—swept aside for a settlement and a smile. As Hubert left, he was tossed one last insult: *"If you have time before your flight, I recommend the Italian restaurant down the street. Try the sausage and peppers."* Ms. Casey gave him a smile

Benjamin left burning with humiliation. *Sausage and peppers,* after all of it.

# CHAPTER 70

Weeks later, Benjamin sat in his office, watching the announcement on TV.

Joyce Donaldson stood at a podium, cameras flashing. "Barclay International and Global Bank & Trust have admitted guilt for failures to safeguard the financial system. They will pay $1.2 billion in fines and $150 million in civil penalties, submit to five years of corporate monitoring, and defer prosecution. Executives will see a portion of their bonuses withheld."

A reporter called out, "Isn't this a slap on the wrist? Five weeks' profit? A speeding ticket?"

Donaldson deflected. Hubert stepped forward, blank-eyed. "We sought a fair settlement that protects the economy. Thank you." He turned and walked away, ignoring the roar of questions.

Benjamin slammed his fist on his desk. Months of work, reduced to performance. He was boiling but beaten.

Charles, watching from home, sagged with relief. "A slap on the hand. Thank you, Emmett..." His voice cracked as he poured a drink, tears spilling where no one could see.

Michael Smithers smirked at the television.

And Emmet Raptnor called his secretary: "Make a reservation at La Perle. Tell my wife to wear her finest. Tonight, she dines with a highly intelligent man."

Camilla, meanwhile, typed a text with trembling fingers: *Julie we need to finish this and find the truth. Library?*

# CHAPTER 71

The library did not fit the upscale beach town around it. Squat, multistoried, and built from salvaged brick, it carried the scent of its own history—charred timbers from the fire that once consumed it lingered in the air like a ghost no amount of polish could banish. Inside, the colors were oddly cheerful, all creams and pastels, as if someone had designed it to resemble an ice cream sundae.

Camilla and Julie hurried up the narrow staircase, their breath quick from both the climb and their mission. Julie, unable to contain herself, announced far too loudly, "Here—this floor looks promising!"

The prim woman at the desk snapped her head up. "Shush! This is a library, not your internet café."

Julie grinned, chastised but unrepentant. "Right, right. Forgot. Old school."

"Where do we even begin?" Camilla asked, staring down the endless aisles of leather-bound spines.

"Divide and conquer. You take the left, I'll take the right," Julie said, slipping into her investigative stride.

Camilla trailed her fingers along the shelves, eyes darting over faded titles. One volume stopped her cold—a thick, worn leather book embossed with markings eerily similar to the one she had bought from Lazlo's shop. Heart quickening, she pulled it free, sank cross-legged onto the floor, and opened to the first fragile page.

Julie, too busy pulling books from her section, didn't notice until Camilla whispered, "Beautiful... fascinating."

"What? Found something?" Julie rushed over and peered down at her. "That doesn't look like Johnny."

"No... but it's about the Gypsies, their instruments, their music. Even Janos Borza is in here." Camilla's voice was hushed, reverent. Then, with a sigh, she closed the cover. "But you're right. I'll check it out for later."

Julie tapped her chin. "We could dig through books forever. What about news archives? They still keep microfiche here, right? The stuff that never makes it online?"

Moments later, they were in a small dimly lit room, the hum of machines filling the silence. Camilla slid into the chair beside Julie, watching her friend crank the reels of film with theatrical flair. Julie's Bogart impression came out in full: "We got a lead, sweetheart. Let's chase it down the old trail..."

Camilla giggled despite herself. Julie always knew how to keep her from drowning in tension.

Twenty minutes later, the laughter had faded. They had nothing but yellowed headlines and dead ends.

"Cammy, think! He must've slipped a name at some point. Maybe in a moment of passion—wink, wink?"

"Ha, you're impossible," Camilla muttered—then froze. A memory surfaced: the oil portrait above Johnny's fireplace, the old man's face she'd admired countless times. She remembered flipping it over when Johnny wasn't looking. There had been a name. A Scottish one.

"Mc... something," she murmured.

"McDuff? McMann? McWho?" Julie teased.

"Shush!" Camilla pressed her temples. Then it clicked. "McTavish. Yes—McTavish."

Julie raised an eyebrow. "Not exactly rare. You remember the first name?"

Camilla's lips curved. "Alban. It was Alban McTavish."

At once she turned back to the machine, scrolling frantically until a grainy photograph froze her in place: an older man at a gravesite, a small boy at his side.

Camilla's breath caught. "That's him. That's Johnny."

Julie leaned close, reading the article aloud.

**Billionaire Alban McTavish, one of the wealthiest men in the world, announced the tragic death of his only daughter, Eloise, and her husband, Richard Oshay. The couple, both stockholders in the McTavish empire, leave behind one young heir to their fortune.**

Camilla covered her mouth, eyes brimming. "His parents... drugs, the crash... That's why he's so against it all. Oh, Johnny..."

Julie let out a low whistle. "Yeah, poor Johnny—the lonely heir to billions."

Camilla turned to her, voice breaking. "Don't you see? This is why he hides. Why he won't live that life. He could have anything, but he chose simplicity. He's nothing like my father." Tears spilled freely now. "Jules, I need to see him. I have to tell him I know."

Julie put a steadying hand on hers. "Not yet. Your dad's mess isn't over. Timing, Cammy. Timing."

Camilla sagged back, torn between love and duty.

Julie, ever quick to lift the mood, gave a sly grin. "Though you have to admit—if your father knew Johnny was a billionaire? All his lecturing about you picking the *right* man would vanish in a second."

Camilla let out a watery laugh, shaking her head. "Oh, the irony."

Together, they walked out of the library, carrying both answers and more questions than ever before.

# CHAPTER 72

Back at home, the library's revelations echoed through Camilla's mind like a song she couldn't silence. Johnny—an heir to one of the world's greatest fortunes. Johnny—the boy in that yellowed newspaper photograph, standing beside a grieving grandfather at a gravesite.

She paced her room, staring at the book she had checked out, its leather cover still carrying the scent of ash and dust. Julie's laughter about her father approving of Johnny *if only he knew* had faded into silence. Camilla wasn't laughing now.

Her phone buzzed on the desk. Messages—dozens of them. Johnny's name filled the screen, each one a fragment of his persistence:

*Camilla, please call me.*

*We need to talk.*

*You know where to find me.*

Her heart pulled toward him, but her father's shadow pressed down heavier. Charles needed her steady. The investigation was swallowing him whole. She couldn't risk adding more chaos.

Julie had been right—timing was everything.

Camilla sank into her chair, pulled her knees to her chest, and whispered into the stillness, "Not yet."

But her fingers trembled as she typed out a message to Julie:

*Jules, you're right. Tell him I'll see him. Not now—but soon. Please make him understand.*

Hitting send, she stared at the ceiling, listening to the faint hum of the house settling around her. Her world had narrowed to two impossible truths: a father who needed her more than ever, and a man who carried secrets that could unravel everything she thought she knew.

And somehow, she would have to find her way between them.

# CHAPTER 73

On the other side of town, Charles stared into his glass of bourbon, the amber liquid trembling with the shake of his hand. The televised announcement still rang in his ears—*deferred prosecution agreement, fines, oversight.* Emmet Raptnor had vanished into his circle of untouchables, untarnished, while Charles was left holding the taste of humiliation.

He leaned back in his leather chair, loosening his tie. His study was dark, the fire guttering in the grate. Relief mingled with despair. Relief that the banks had escaped true punishment. Despair that his own life would never be the same.

On the desk beside him lay a photo of Viola, her silk scarf caught mid-motion in a breeze from years past. Camilla had worn a scarf so like it the other night. He'd almost lost his temper then, but tonight he clung to the memory of his daughter's eyes, loyal in spite of everything.

He whispered into the silence, "Viola, I'm trying. She's all I have left. Don't let me lose her too."

Upstairs, Camilla whispered too—words her father would never hear.

"Johnny, I miss you. But not yet... not yet."

Their voices never reached each other, but the air in the house carried both confessions: a father afraid of losing his daughter, and a daughter afraid of losing the man she loved.

# CHAPTER 74

Hopping on one foot, Johnny rushed around his loft looking for his missing shoe. "Where the heck is that shoe?" He spotted it half-buried under the bed, tugged it free, slipped it on, and bolted toward the door. At the last second, he remembered his phone. Snatching it from the table, he saw Camilla's name glowing across the screen.

His heart leapt. *She wrote back.*

He began to dial, then froze. This wasn't a conversation he could rush through on his way out the door. He was already late for his grandfather. Instead, he typed quickly, pouring every ounce of urgency into his fingers:

*So happy. Can't wait to see you again too. On my way to Grandfather's now. Please come over in two hours—I'll be back, I promise. hugs and kisses* ❤️

He sent it, started the car, and sped off, Camilla's face filling his thoughts until the Ridgemont's stone façade appeared ahead.

Inside, Nurse Paulson intercepted him, pulling him toward a quiet corner of the recreation room. On the couch sat his grandfather, beside a stooped but dignified man with watery eyes and trembling hands.

"Johnny," the man said warmly, extending his hand. "I'm so happy to finally meet you."

Johnny looked to his grandfather, unsure. Alban gave a small nod. "He knows. I told him you're painting his daughter."

The man's voice cracked as he spoke again. "I cannot describe what that means to me. To see her again, even through your art... it brings warmth to my heart."

Johnny sat down, humbled. "Milosh, I'm honored. The painting is close to finished, but something's missing. I can see her beauty, her kindness, but there's a loneliness I don't yet understand. If you can—please, tell me her story. I need to feel her the way she truly lived."

Milosh's eyes drifted to Alban, who placed a hand on his shoulder. "It may help you to share it, old friend. And it may help Johnny, too."

So Milosh began, his words trembling but steady:

"We came from former Yugoslavia, simple people with simple lives. My wife cooked for the wealthy; I worked their gardens. Our daughter... she was our pride. Then she met a man far above our station, but he loved her, and she adored him. We stepped aside to let her fly higher than we ever could. She had a child, a little girl. From afar, we watched them both grow."

His hands twisted together. "But when I signed away our home to Charles Huntington, promising her a better life, I gave away more than bricks and walls. I gave away her freedom."

Johnny's stomach knotted. *Camilla's father.*

Milosh pressed on, tears brimming. "She came back to me once, desperate. Said her marriage had soured. She was slapped, silenced, but never stopped protecting her daughter. She asked me to hide her costumes so she could dance with the theater troupe. For weeks, she came alive again—laughing, moving, free. I thought perhaps we had her back."

His voice broke. "Then one night, I found her beaten and stabbed outside the theater. I held her as she bled. She begged me not to blame Charles. She said, 'He will protect our girl. Let him.' And then she was gone."

Silence filled the room. Even Alban's stoic eyes glistened.

Johnny felt every word settle into him like pigment into canvas. The sorrow, the fleeting joy, the sacrifice all of it gave him the missing thread for his painting. "Thank you, Milosh. Now I can finish. I promise, I'll honor her."

Milosh nodded, reaching into his pocket. He drew out a small velvet pouch with a gold drawstring. "This is for you. Payment."

Johnny shook his head. "No—you've given me enough. Your trust, your story..."

"Please." Milosh pressed it into his hands. "Open it."

Inside, nestled in silk, was a white-gold ring. Its band was etched with delicate scrollwork, and five blossoms shimmered on its crown: two violets studded with diamonds, two more with amethyst, and a single yellow citrine burning at the center like captured sunlight.

Johnny's breath caught. "Milosh, this must be priceless—"

"It was hers," Milosh whispered. "Someday you'll know who deserves it. Promise me you'll pass it to the right one."

Johnny closed his fist around the ring, the metal cool against his skin. "I promise."

He looked back once before leaving, watching the two old men clasp hands, their grief binding them tighter than blood. And as he stepped into the cool evening air, the velvet pouch in his pocket, Johnny knew the painting would never be just paint on canvas. It would be her resurrection.

Johnny knew he could finish the painting now; Milosh's story had given him the missing threads—joy, heartbreak, and sacrifice woven together.

Yet, instead of rushing home to capture it all, he lingered. Something in Milosh's eyes told him there was more. He walked back into the recreation room and approached Milosh.

"But Milosh" Johnny asked gently, "how did you end up here at Ridgemont? It's... well, it's exclusive. And expensive."

Milosh's gaze grew distant, his voice low. "After Viollca died, I had to tell my wife. I couldn't bear to do it in our home, so I suggested a walk along the old stone bridge—our special place." His throat tightened. "We were halfway across when headlights came out of nowhere. A car tore onto the walkway, swerving wildly, the roar of its engine echoing against the stone. It all happened so fast. She was thrown over the railing, into the river below."

His hands trembled as if still reaching for her. "Later, I learned whose car it was. A drunk driver—your parents, Johnny. Their night of excess became the end of my wife's life."

Johnny's breath caught, his stomach twisting. The story he'd grown up hearing—that his parents lost control of their car and plunged into the river—suddenly took on new horror. They hadn't only killed themselves. Their reckless crash had stolen Milosh's wife as well.

Milosh's eyes softened, the bitterness in his tone giving way to sorrow. "I wanted to follow her. I climbed onto the ledge. I was ready to let go."

His voice faltered. "And then your grandfather appeared. Alban pulled me back with a strength I didn't know an old man could have. He held me while I wept, whispering, *'I will take care of you. Together, we will heal.'*"

Johnny stared at Milosh, his pulse racing, his skin clammy. He finally understood. The bond between Alban and Milosh wasn't simply friendship; it was forged from shared loss, a wound that had never truly closed.

As he turned to leave, he looked back one last time. The two old men sat shoulder to shoulder, tears and laughter mingling in the same breath, grief transforming into a fragile form of peace.

Johnny's heart hammered. He had no time to waste. The images, the emotions, the weight of Milosh's confession—they burned in him like fire. He sprinted through the Ridgemont's glass doors, barely remembering to wave goodbye to Nurse Paulson. Racing to his car, he fumbled with the keys, his thoughts consumed by color, form, and expression.

"This is it," he muttered. "This is the truth she's been hiding in her eyes."

He sped back to his loft, every second vital, afraid the intensity of what he felt might fade. He threw his coat to the floor, grabbed his brushes, and attacked the canvas. With every stroke, grief and love poured into the portrait—his parents' mistakes, Milosh's sacrifice, his grandfather's compassion. Johnny painted feverishly, needing to finish while the story still pulsed through his veins.

The sadness in the woman's eyes finally deepened into truth, layered with resilience and a fragile beauty that could only be born of loss.

When he finally stepped back, breathless, his hands trembling, Johnny whispered, "Now... now you're real."

<h1 style="text-align:center">CHAPTER 75</h1>

Sitting in his office with a drink in hand, Charles let the relief wash over him. They had walked away from Washington with little more than a slap on the wrist. Lucky. Too lucky. But the thought nagged at him, circling back to the man who had always been there in the shadows, stirring up as much trouble as he solved: Michael Smithers.

Charles pressed the intercom. "Sylvia, get me Michael Smithers. Now."

Minutes later, Michael strolled in, his grin wide, his cologne filling the room before he even sat down. He eyed the glass in Charles's hand. "Hey, I'll take one of those too. Time to celebrate, ole man!"

"Don't *ole man* me," Charles muttered, his jaw tight.

Michael laughed. "What's up? We came out alive and with all our teeth. I'd say we won."

Charles's eyes hardened. "That's just it. I was starting to feel the same... until I realized what always follows you. Trouble. More trouble than I can afford. What other hell are you going to drag me into next, Michael?"

Michael leaned back in his chair, smirking. "Oh, come on, Charles. We've been through thick and thin. You're aiming your anger at the wrong man." His grin widened, wicked now. "Why don't you go home and slap your daughter around instead?"

Charles slammed his glass down so hard amber liquid splashed across the desk. "You bastard! I've had it with you." His voice trembled with rage. "I called you in to tell you—you're done. Fired. Sylvia typed up your notice as soon as the announcement aired. You've got six weeks' pay and last month's bonus. Take it and get out." He shoved the sealed envelope across the desk.

Michael opened it leisurely, chuckling as he scanned the paper. "Generous, I'll give you that. So what's it going to be—let me walk out on my own, or send me off with the guards?"

"Don't push me," Charles growled.

Michael's eyes glinted with malice. "After all the messes I cleaned up for you, this is how you repay me? You think your hands are clean? You're as dirty as I am, Charles. You just liked pretending you weren't the one in the mud." He leaned forward, lowering his voice. "You deserved that tramp you married, and she deserved what she got. That's one mess I'm proud of cleaning up."

Charles froze. "Wha—what did you say?"

Michael grinned wider, savoring the shock on Charles's face. "Don't act so innocent. Remember that day you came to me, moaning about how maybe marrying her was a mistake? You opened that door, Charles. You asked me to help."

Charles's voice cracked. "No... I only confided in you. I was upset and distracted. I *never* wanted—what did you do?"

Michael shrugged, casual, cruel. "I tried to... soften her up a bit. She rejected me. So I called in a favor. They were only supposed to rough her up. Scare her. But she fought back. She was fiery, your Viola. Too fiery. Things got... messy. Oops. One more tramp off the streets."

Charles staggered back, bile rising in his throat. His hands trembled, reaching for the desk for balance.

Michael raised a bottle from the sideboard like a weapon, realizing he'd pushed too far.

But Charles pressed the intercom with deadly calm. "Sylvia, did you get all that?"

"Yes, sir," Sylvia's voice crackled through. "And I have security here ready."

Two guards strode in, each grabbing one of Michael's arms.

Michael struggled, sneering as he was dragged toward the door. "Three little words, Charles—statute of limitations. You've got nothing. Nothing!"

Charles's voice cut like steel. "With your arrogance, you'll hang yourself sooner or later. And I will be there to make sure of it."

"Get him out," he barked, his face pale, his body shaking.

The office door slammed behind them.

Charles collapsed into his chair, trembling so violently Sylvia rushed in. "Mr. Huntington, are you all right? Should I call 911?"

"No... no," Charles whispered, his voice hoarse. "Just... too much today."

She touched his shoulder gently. "Then go home, sir. Rest. I'll take care of everything here."

Charles nodded faintly, his mind a storm. Viola's face swam before his eyes, not as a vague memory of regret but vivid, raw, and bloody. He had spent years wondering, punishing himself silently, burying the doubt. And now Michael had given him the answer.

The truth.

The horror.

And the unbearable knowledge that he had let it all happen.

# CHAPTER 76

The brush moved almost of its own accord, as though Viola herself guided his hand. Johnny leaned into the canvas, layering light and shadow, sorrow and hope, until her face began to breathe again through the paint. Every detail Milosh had told him surged into the strokes—the joy of stolen hours with her parents, the secret dances, the fear, the betrayal, the love for her daughter and the faint whisper *"Let the colors bring you life"*

When at last his hand stilled, he staggered back, chest heaving. Viola's eyes stared back at him—alive with fire, rimmed with sorrow, whispering truths he wasn't sure he was ready to hear.

The smell of turpentine and oil clung to him. His throat burned with thirst. He reached for the coffee pot, only to find it empty. "Damn," he muttered, rubbing his temples. Too drained to care about appearances, he pulled on his coat over his paint-stained shirt and slipped into the street, heading down to the corner café. The chill in the air cleared his head, but the weight of the painting still pressed against his ribs.

# CHAPTER 77

Meanwhile, Charles sat in the back of his limo, Michael's words replaying in his skull like a death knell. Viola's face. Her laughter. Her silken scarf. And Michael's mocking voice:

*She deserved what she got.*

His hand shook as he poured another drink, but the burn no longer dulled the edges. Nothing would ever dull them again.

At last, he told the driver to take him home. He needed something solid, someone to anchor him before he unraveled completely. Camilla. His daughter.

The house loomed silent as he pushed through the front doors, calling her name. "Camilla?" Only Paola appeared in the hall, wringing her hands.

"Señor, she is not here. She went out some time ago."

Charles's chest tightened. He turned toward the stairs, the empty silence echoing like a rebuke. He had come home for comfort and found only absence.

In the café down the street, Johnny ordered a black coffee, his mind already racing back to Viola's eyes on the canvas. At the same moment, Charles poured another drink in his study, staring at his reflection in the darkened window.

Two men, both haunted by the same woman's ghost.

# CHAPTER 78

Checking the TV room, office, and finally her bedroom, Charles could not find her anywhere. The house was too quiet, its silence pressing in on him. Desperation gnawed at his insides. He even checked Camilla's closet and bathroom—places he hadn't entered since she was a child. Clothes lay tossed across the chair, makeup scattered across the dressing table. She had left in haste, and that haste made Charles suspicious.

*Where are you? Where did you go? That boy.*

Snatching his coat, he stormed down the stairs. Paola appeared from the kitchen, drying her hands on her apron. "Señor, what do you want me to tell Camilla if I see her?"

But Charles barreled past, ignoring her words, his polished shoes striking like gunshots on the marble floor as he shoved open the front door.

He found himself driving aimlessly until his instincts brought him to a place he hadn't seen in over a decade: the narrow street where the old repair shop stood. The sign was faded now, the windows grimy with time, but stepping inside was like walking back into another life. The air smelled faintly of machine oil and cedar. The sensation was immediate and visceral—*déjà vu.*

Behind the counter stood a man Charles instantly recognized despite the passing years. His face was more lined, his hair now gray, but the eyes were unchanged. Loiza.

The older man froze for a heartbeat, his gaze locking with Charles's. His expression flickered from recognition to shock, and then to something more guarded. "Charles," he said quietly. "Been a very long time."

Charles didn't bother with pleasantries. "Where is he? Where is that boy you're helping? Bring him to me right now."

Loiza's eyes narrowed. His voice, though soft, carried steel. "My heartfelt sympathy for all you have endured, Charles. But remember— I am not one of your domestics. Do not order me."

The words stung. For an instant, Charles faltered. Memories of Loiza's kindness surfaced—how he had once helped Viola, how he had been a silent ally when others turned away.

Charles softened, lowering his voice. "Of course not. But I have a serious situation here, and I'm asking for your help. Please."

Loiza studied him a long moment, then inclined his head slightly. "Help, yes. But on my terms, Charles."

He shifted his gaze past Charles's shoulder. Charles followed the look—and froze.

A young man was walking briskly behind him toward the stairway to the loft. Broad shoulders. Brown hair. The posture of someone both confident and restless.

Loiza saw the recognition dawn in Charles's eyes. He placed a hand on the counter and spoke with quiet conviction.

"Charles, you know my loyalty has always been to family. Nothing else matters. Your family's love is what will save you if you don't throw it away. A daughter's love is sacred—hold onto that. Think of her."

Then he gestured toward the stairwell. "He is up those stairs. His name is Johnny."

# CHAPTER 79

Charles's pulse hammered in his temples. Loiza's words still echoed—*A daughter's love is sacred.* But his eyes were locked on the stairwell, where the shadow of the young man disappeared upward, each step creaking faintly.

Johnny.

The name burned in his mind.

Charles clenched his fists, every nerve alive with fury, suspicion, and something else he dared not name—fear. Fear of losing his daughter. Fear of facing truths he had kept buried.

Loiza leaned on the counter, his gaze steady, almost sorrowful. "He is up those stairs, Charles. But remember what I said—think of her."

Charles's breath caught in his throat. He took one step toward the stairs. And another.

The air seemed heavier, charged with something inevitable, like the seconds before a storm breaks.

Halfway up, he paused, looking back at Loiza. The old man stood in silence, his face unreadable.

Charles turned forward again, his hand gripping the rail so tightly his knuckles turned white.

One more step, and the creak of the wood seemed louder than a gunshot.

At the top of the stairs... waited the boy.

# CHAPTER 80

Johnny flung his coat and keys onto the love seat. The canvas waited for him where he'd left it. With reverent hands, he removed the protective black cheesecloth. Palette clutched like a shield, he attacked the canvas with fevered precision, each stroke deliberate yet urgent. The woman's face emerged beneath his brush—eyes gaining depth, lips curving with secrets. A strange mist arose around the painting and seemed to hover at the edges of his vision.

*"Let the colors bring you life,"* came a whisper, so delicate he nearly missed it. Instead of doubting, he surrendered to the voice, letting it guide his hand. The outside world fell away. With the voice growing stronger, he channeled both his emotions and hers through each brushstroke. He was adding the final highlights to her eyes when a knock shattered his concentration, but he couldn't stop. With one last, decisive stroke, he completed the finishing touch to the portrait.

Quickly, he draped the black cheesecloth back over the canvas, concealing his work before answering the knock.

"Oh, Camilla, you are early!" He ran over to open the door, anxious to see her face, but instead he found himself looking at a quite different face.

"Um, hello... May I help you?" he asked Charles.

Charles pushed him aside and walked in, scouting the place. "Where is she? Where is my daughter?"

"Oh, you are Mr. Huntington, Camilla's father. It is nice to m—"
But before he could finish, Charles was in the kitchen, yanking open
drawers agitatedly.

"Excuse me, what are you looking for?" Johnny tried to stop him.

"Get away from me! I am finding anything of hers to know she was
here." Opening a drawer, Charles spotted the check.

"Mr. Huntington, I am not denying your daughter has been here,
many times, but she is not here now." Johnny tried to calm him down,
only to have the check shoved in his face.

"Where did you get this?" Charles demanded.

"A Michael Smithers gave it to me to, um, to go away."

"Why haven't you cashed it?" Charles shoved the check at Johnny
again. "Cash it and go away!"

"No, sir, respectfully, I don't—" But the more Johnny tried to
communicate, the more upset Charles became. Consumed with anger
and hatred, Charles lashed out, physically attacking him.

But he was no match for a strong young man, especially in his
weakened condition. Johnny easily overcame him, knocking him to the
ground. As Johnny tried to help him back up, the door flew open, and
both men froze. Camilla stood there, tears in her eyes.

"Father, Johnny, what is going on?"

"Camilla, your boyfriend was just about to take this very large
check..." Charles tried to twist the story, but Camilla knew better.

"Dad, that is not true. Johnny would never take the check. He
doesn't need the money; he has a trust fund that is hundreds of times
the amount of that check," Camilla snapped.

"How... how did you know?" Johnny asked, stunned.

"It is ok, Johnny... I just know." She ran into his arms. "You are a good man, I know you."

Turning back to her father, she said, "Dad, please. Johnny is a good man, a giving man. I've been up here a lot because he is an artist. See, he is painting my portrait."

And before Johnny could stop her, Camilla pulled off the cheesecloth, thinking it was her painting, only to reveal the portrait of her mother.

Charles staggered backward at the sight, knees buckling. The face that had haunted his dreams for a decade now stared back at him from Johnny's canvas—those eyes, luminous and knowing. His fingers trembled as he reached toward the painting without touching it.

"Viollca," he whispered, his voice cracking on her name. "My sweet flower."

The room seemed to fill with the scent of her perfume—lilacs and rain. And somewhere between memory and miracle, he could have sworn he heard her whisper: *Let the colors bring you life.*

When he finally rose, his face was wet, his breathing ragged, but something long frozen inside him had begun to thaw.

Camilla's hand flew to her mouth. "That's—that's my mother," she whispered.

Johnny nodded softly. "I realized it weeks ago. The resemblance is unmistakable—those eyes especially. The same depth, the same light. It's why I was trying so hard to see you and talk to you."

Camilla's fingers trembled as she reached toward the canvas without touching it. "But how did you... where did you..."

"I painted her for someone named Milosh—a friend of my grandfather's."

"Milosh Borza?" Charles's voice cut through, sharp with recognition.

"Yes, that's him," Johnny confirmed.

Camilla turned to her father; confusion etched on her face. "Who is Milosh?"

Charles steadied himself against the wall, his handkerchief damp with tears. "Milosh Borza is your mother's father," he said, the words heavy with unspoken history. "A man I've wronged beyond measure."

As he stared at the portrait, the air around him seemed to vibrate with an invisible melody, a violin playing ever so softly. And he could almost hear Viollca's voice carried on the phantom music: *"Let the music open your heart."*

Charles and Camilla stood transfixed, warmth radiating through them like sunlight. The portrait of Viollca worked something inexplicable in them both—a healing neither could articulate but both unmistakably felt.

A soft voice echoing *"let the colors bring you life"*

Charles turned to his daughter, newfound strength flowing through him, and pulled her into a tight embrace.

The door opened. Loiza entered, his weathered face softening at the sight.

"At last, my niece knows the truth," he said.

Camilla blinked. "Niece?"

"Milosh is my brother," Loiza explained, then turned to Johnny. "Your grandfather arranged for you to rent my loft so I could watch over you—repayment for his kindness to Milosh. After losing Viollca and then his wife, Milosh was broken. Your grandfather saved him, hiding him away in comfort all these years—benefactor, protector, angel. Heaven awaits such a man."

Johnny nodded. "Yes, I know... but they healed each other."

Charles approached Loiza with an outstretched hand. "Can you forgive me? All these years I had the means but never helped."

"I'm not the one you need to ask," Loiza replied simply.

Charles's shoulders slumped. "What can I possibly say to him after everything?"

"You'll find the words," Camilla said, squeezing his arm. "Look into Mother's eyes for strength—the same strength that's healing us now."

Charles hesitated. "But how do I even begin—" A smile bloomed across Camilla's face, something ancient stirring in her own Romani blood.

Charles hesitated, his throat tight. "But how do I face him after all these years?"

Camilla's eyes were gleaming with a strength that startled him. For an instant, Charles swore he saw another presence shining through her—the same unshakable spirit that had once danced in Viollca's eyes.

"Father," she said softly but with unwavering certainty, "I know exactly what to do." She reached for his hand, steadying him, her grip firm with resolve. "Come—we have preparations to make."

Johnny, still hovering near the veiled canvas, exchanged a glance with Loiza. Neither spoke. Both knew the tide had shifted. The ghost of the past was no longer content to linger in the shadow—through Camilla, she was demanding reckoning, and perhaps at last, redemption.

# CHAPTER 81

The rusted hinges of the cemetery gates groaned as they parted, unveiling a centuries-old path where rose petals blanketed worn cobblestones, a fragrant carpet for the mourners' procession.

At the head came a horse-drawn carriage draped with ribbons and flowers, sunlight catching on the metal trim, scattering shards of light across the path. Faces familiar and new lined the way—some smiling faintly in anticipation, others holding grief in their eyes. Julie stood with her family, waving gently, while further down the artist's alley folk, dressed in bold colors and layered fabrics, leaned in with reverent curiosity.

Hempshaw and Milosh walked arm-in-arm, their heads bent together, old voices trading memories. Just behind them Alban followed at his own slow pace, smiling as he watched the two brothers reunite after so many years.

Hempshaw turned, his voice low but steady. "Thank you for taking care of my brother all these years."

Alban replied with equal weight. "I think he took care of me. And thank you—for looking after my grandson."

A few steps behind, Charles's stride faltered at the sight of them all together. His dark suit clung heavily to his shoulders, his breaths sharp, as though every step forward cost him something. On either side, Johnny and Camilla kept pace, their presence a quiet anchor.

"Dad, breathe," Camilla whispered, slipping her hand into his. Warmth spread from her touch, steadying his trembling fingers.

Milosh broke away from the line and approached. His steps carried dignity, his expression softening as he reached Charles. "This means more than you know," he said.

Charles opened his mouth, voice unsteady "After everything I—"

But Milosh laid a hand on his shoulder, silencing him with gentle weight. "Today is our beginning," he said simply. "Viola would have wanted it this way."

Then reaching over and lifting Camillas left hand he leaned over and gave her ring finger a gentle kiss, admiring the ring on her finger, white-gold, a band etched with delicate scrollwork, five blossoms on its crown: two violets studded with diamonds, two more with amethyst, and a single yellow citrine burning at the center.

"It fits you perfectly and your mother would be very pleased" Milosh said as he admired the fit of the ring.

Then looking over to Johnny he nodded a thank you.

Johnny, carrying the violin case, nodded back and then glanced at Camilla. At her nod, he opened the case and presented the instrument. She tucked it beneath her chin, a quiet smile flickering across her lips, one she saved only for her father. The first notes rose—low, aching, a funeral dirge that threaded through the cool morning air, both mournful and strangely hopeful. She led the procession forward, the melody carrying them to Viola's memorial.

The portrait rested on an ornate stand above the veiled gravestone. As Camilla's bow carved deeper into the strings, the music shifted— transforming into a bright Romani tune, full of fire and freedom, drawing the crowd closer. Her bow danced, her body moving with the rhythm until, finally, the last high note trembled into silence.

Standing before her mother's likeness, Camilla smiled through her tears.

Charles stepped closer, voice breaking with awe. "I remember you playing as a child, but I had no idea you were so... so gifted." His eyes flicked from Camilla to the portrait, recognition dawning. He hugged her tightly.

Turning to the crowd, Charles raised his voice, steadier than he felt. "Thank you all for being here today. We have come to honor Viola's spirit in the Romani way." He gestured toward the portrait, its painted eyes luminous. "Though we cannot lay her body to rest, Johnny has given us something perhaps more precious—her essence, captured forever in oils and canvas."

His throat tightened, but he looked directly at Johnny and mouthed the words *thank you.*

"I believe it is only right," Charles continued, "that Viollca's father lead us in the ritual."

Milosh stepped forward. His weathered face softened as he gazed at his daughter's likeness. "Our tradition asks that we seek forgiveness from those who have passed," he explained. "I will begin, and then others may follow. Charles and Camilla"—he nodded toward them—"will complete the circle."

He leaned closely into Viola's portrait whispering to his daughter words no one else could hear. For an instant, his lips curved into a smile, as if she had answered him. Behind him, mourners approached one by one, murmuring apologies and remembrances to the portrait.

Camilla came next, her breath shallow. She bent close, her lips barely grazing the canvas. "I should have kept playing," she whispered, a tear slipping down her cheek. For the briefest moment, the painted eyes seemed to glow, and she thought she heard violin strings hum from within the frame.

Charles followed last. His shoulders sagged beneath the weight of years, his voice rough with shame. "I failed at so much," he whispered. "But I can begin again, here and now." He looked at Milosh, then back at Viola's face. "Viola, my love, , for the years of refusing to understand, forgive me for the years of silence, forgive me for silencing your music. Words are not enough. Let me show you instead."

Together—Charles, Johnny, Milosh, Hempshaw, and Alban— pulled away the heavy shroud, revealing the gleaming marble gravestone beneath. Carved into its polished surface were violets intertwined with a bow and violin, gleaming in the sunlight.

"This," Charles whispered, "is the tribute you always deserved."

Camilla's hands trembled on the violin. "All these years, Dad, you made me choose. But look around us. "Music never lessened the weight of business, nor art the strength of order. Together they became one heartbeat, and in that union, we were stronger."

Something inside Charles broke open, and with it came a strange peace. His eyes filled, but his face softened into gratitude. He turned to the gravestone and read aloud the inscription etched there:

**VIOLA BORZA HUNTINGTON**

*January 5, 1965 – February 10, 1998*

His voice wavered—until, impossibly, another voice joined his own. Viola's soprano, faint but unmistakable, braided with his baritone:

*Let the music open your heart.*

*Let the colors bring you life.*

*Let the dance set you free.*

And then, Charles froze. For there, shimmering in the light behind Camilla, stood Viola—soft, radiant, not quite flesh but no longer just memory. Their eyes met across the veil of life and death. A smile touched her lips, and for the first time in decades, Charles felt himself smile in return. Her form shimmering like morning mist, then rose and dissolved into the sky, leaving only music behind.

# EPILOGUE

The music opened their hearts, the colors brought them life, and the dance set them free. Though the portrait was still, its legacy moved like breath through generations. For in that silence lived love, forgiveness, and the promise of new beginnings.